I0457065

Lok's Love

An Alien Exchange, Volume 5

Keri Kruspe

Published by StarChance Publications, 2024.

This is a work of fiction. Similarities to real people, places, or events are entirely coincidental.

LOK'S LOVE

First edition. February 14, 2024.

Copyright © 2024 Keri Kruspe.

ISBN: 979-8987372685

Written by Keri Kruspe.

Table of Contents

Chapter One

In the dimly lit confines of the *StarChance* spaceship's cramped bathroom, Althea MacGregor peered at the mist-covered mirror. Her reflection seemed to whisper a question that echoed through her mind. How had she, an aging nobody in her forties, land herself on the precipice of the most breathtaking adventure imaginable?

After enduring countless heartbreaks and setbacks, Althea seized on the unexpected opportunity to transcend her mundane existence. Among the countless women populating the world, fate placed her in the elite ranks of a select few women embarking on a voyage into the vast unknown—a daring alien-exchange program, with the tantalizing promise of discovering true love among the stars.

As the sound of the spaceship engines hummed in the background, Althea's pulse quickened with anticipation. The confines of her past crumbled away, replaced by the boundless potential now before her. This was her chance to redefine herself. To leave behind the disaster of her former life for something better.

Althea clenched her fingers so she wouldn't pinch herself, just to make sure she wasn't dreaming. It boggled her mind that she'd had the courage to sign up for the alien-exchange program in the first place. But here she was, in a tiny cabin aboard an honest-to-God spaceship, racing toward an alien planet. And all without getting kidnapped like the heroines in her favorite sci-fi romances, thank you very much.

A slight ping rang in the outer bedroom. She gave her reflection a quick once-over to make sure she looked the best she could. Her dark-brown, shoulder-length tresses were glossy and smooth. Check. Brown eyes accentuated with light mascara on her lashes and her eyebrows touched up with a subtle hint of color. Check. Light, neutral lip gloss. Not too bold, not too invisible. Check. She smoothed her palms over the tan trousers that coordinated with her pale-peach blouse and gave her pasty skin a bit of a glow. With one last reassuring smile at her reflection, she nodded. Damn, she was as ready as she'd ever be.

She waved a hand over the bedroom door's controls, and the panel slid open to reveal a surprise.

Aja, the liaison between the small group of humans on the ship and the Zerin aliens who ran it, stood there.

No matter how amiable Aja acted, from the beginning, the pretty alien made Althea uncomfortable.

"Are you ready to go, Althea?" Aja had her hands behind herself, her head tilted, and wore a stiff smile. Her wine-red hair was tucked into a tight weave, leaving a tail of braids that ended at the back of her thighs. With her hair pulled back, it left her face bare and highlighted her pointy ears decorated with multi-colored crystal earrings dangling in a single rope from the tips, ending an inch above each lobe. Her dual-colored irises were another hint of her alien nature. The first ring of color in their almond-shape was a dark shade of greenish yellow followed by a light shade of khaki. Her long, thick lashes matched her rich eyebrows, the same burgundy as her illustrious hair. Her porcelain-smooth skin with its underlying honey tint now flushed.

Althea's eyes widened at what Aja wore. Holy shit! What? Was the female going to fight some superhero somewhere?

Instead of her normal uniform of a one-piece, cream-colored suit, the liaison had on a bizarre outfit that would be right at home in any comic-book movie. The form-fitting outfit shimmered whenever she moved. Over her chest was a silver plate decorated with swirls that matched those on her wristbands.

Wow, those babies had to be at least two inches wide and would give Wonder Woman a run for her money.

On her feet were a pair of black leather boots that reached over her knees. The steel over the toes bore the same pattern as her chest plate. A shimmering cape flowed dramatically behind her to the top of her butt. Its slight silver brought out the glittering colors of her suit and accessories. The strangest thing she had on was something that looked like a tip of a spear poking up between her shoulder blades. What in the hell was she going to do with that? In all the training they'd attended about the Exchange over the last thirty days, Aja never hinted it might be dangerous.

Aja didn't say anything. She just grasped one of Althea's hands and tapped the wrist with her thumb.

A sharp pinch on the skin there made Althea's breath catch. She tried to yank her hand back, but Aja's grip was too tight.

"No, you don't." The alien woman leaned close. "Just give it a minute, and let it do its thing, as you humans like to say." Her plump lips creased into a sneer. "And you will follow me as if you're happy to do so."

Althea's mood went from giddy excitement to massive confusion so fast it made her head spin. What did Aja say? Follow her? Where? She didn't want to go anywhere. That floor looked like the perfect place to take a nap. Damn, why was she so lethargic? Did that freaking woman drug her? Well, crap. That wasn't necessary. She couldn't wait to get to the Exchange. Didn't she prove it by leaving everything on Earth behind to follow the Zerins into outer space?

She tried to open her mouth to ask her questions, but nothing happened. Someone had turned off her vocal cords. Jeez, her mouth must be disconnected from her brain. The more she tried to struggle against the sensation, the more her stomach swam in an acidic bath.

Aja yanked at her with a narrow-eyed glare. She looked deep into Althea's eyes. "Yep, you're ready. Come on, bitch. Let's go."

Another harsh tug, and Althea meekly stumbled next to Aja into the now-crowded corridor of excited human women laughing with excitement. The crowd headed in one direction while she and Aja traipsed the opposite way. Boy, this must be how a salmon felt when they fought upstream to spawn. Good thing most women walked around them, even though a lot of them turned their heads and watched as they passed by. But with Aja being a prominent figure on the ship, no one stopped them.

Althea's lips were numb, along with her hands, and there was a tingling sensation on her feet. Maybe she'd get lucky and her legs would give out and make her fall ass first onto the hard floor. Hah! What would the stupid alien bitch do then? Carry her? Aja may have been tall for a female, at just under six feet, but Althea was no slouch in the height department herself. At five foot eight, she had a healthy weight of around one-fifty. She giggled. Okay, maybe that number might be a teeny, tiny little lie. But, still... If she passed out, maybe then she'd be lucky enough Aja would just leave her on the floor and forget all about her. Getting trampled by an excited herd of human woman would be better than whatever Aja had in mind. No doubt it was something Althea'd rather avoid.

Damn and hellfire. Trust her to get abducted by aliens anyway.

* * *

Several weeks later, on the slave planet FiPan - deep in the bowels of a prison complex in the lair of Dred Pirate Maynwaring

"Do you think it'll ever come back online?"

Althea glanced at Lisa, her fellow inmate, before looking back at the robot on the other side of the force field. Since the question was a rhetorical one for the umpteenth time, she didn't bother to answer. Nothing had changed for hours now. She studied the strange, neon-red android shaped like a bald human woman. That is, if the woman had three huge double D boobs.

Damn cyborg gave Barbie a run for her money on being a young boy's wet dream. Right now, the stupid thing just stood there, her metallic hand eerily frozen in action before disengaging the force field that held Althea, Lisa, and three other women hostages in a smelly prison cell. None of them had a clue why the robot froze like that. Freakin' robot could've had the decency to shut off the shimmering force field first.

"I wonder if it being frozen like that is a good thing?" Lisa mused with her arms crossed and her honey-colored eyes narrowed. "Or a bad one."

"Yeah." Althea put her hands on her hips. "Well, let's look at it this way. If she's stuck like that, we don't have to worry about her taking us to the sellers' block like she did the others. But the bad news is, if someone doesn't come soon, we'll starve to death. We haven't seen anyone since that stupid thing froze like that yesterday." She spoke in a hushed voice, hoping the other women in the cell didn't hear her. Not that it mattered. Pretty sure they were all smart enough to figure out the obvious situation with no help from her.

Lisa grunted.

Althea put her hands behind her back and studied the unmoving robot... cyborg... android... whatever...on the other side. What she wouldn't give to get her hands on the thing to take it apart. She might not have had any formal mechanical training, but she loved to dismantle things to see how they worked. If she couldn't do that, maybe there was a way for her to reach it with one of those weapon thingies around the robot's trim waist. Too bad the only way to do that was to put her hand through the force field. She snorted. Like she'd do something that asinine again. The first and only time she barely touched the damn thing, it burned the tip of her finger. Now a blood blister the size of a dime throbbed. She crossed her arms to stop from picking at it to make it pop. The last thing she needed was to let it get infected.

With a regretful sigh, she turned and gazed around the cage, studying the faces of the other captives. "We might as well sit down and relax. Doesn't look like anything's going to happen any time soon."

Althea studied the other three hostages, who were either asleep or staring at nothing with dead eyes. Each one of them had been part of the Alien Exchange program that was supposed to lead them to the love of their lives. And the same alien bitch who deceived her betrayed all of them. Aja.

Lisa nodded and gave Althea's hand a tight squeeze.

Althea smiled back, but couldn't bring herself to say anything. What was there to say, anyway?

She sat on the cold, hard floor with Lisa beside her. Well, wasn't this just peachy? Here they were, locked in a prison cell for what seemed like forever. She bent one knee and rested an elbow on it, blindly looking around. Heh, the only thing to look forward to was the gift of increasing dread, with a heaping sense of helplessness mixed in. Might as well top the whole thing off with a sprinkling of panic.

Normally, she'd force herself not to wallow in negative emotions. And not let anyone else tell her what she could or couldn't do. If she had, she'd have died a long time ago. She might not want to change her strong-willed outlook on life anytime soon, but it wouldn't be the first time her stubborn attitude pushed everyone away. Loneliness might be a bitch, but at least the emotion was a constant companion.

Althea put both feet flat on the floor and wrapped her arms around her legs, drawing them to her chest. With a sigh she pressed her forehead against her knees. Just her luck, she left Earth only to be stuck in this stinking shithole to rot.

For the umpteenth time, she'd tried to do something different to improve her lot in life. And every damn time, it turned sideways. Now she was here in this cramped cell where the walls were too thick and the force field too strong. Her only option was to sit and wait for God knew what.

She must've dozed off because an unusual, distant sound jerked her awake. It was faint, but different from anything she'd heard before. "What's that?" Her heart skipped a beat. She jumped up and rushed towards the shivering opening.

"What's what?" Lisa skidded next to her. "You think a dimensional portal is being activated? I've always wanted to go through one!"

Althea raised her eyebrows at her companion. As a science-fiction-romance writer, Lisa came up with the weirdest scenarios.

"What are you guys looking at?" Toni from LA asked.

An excited squeal came from Izzy, a librarian from New York State. "Someone's coming?"

Morgan, the reigning critic of the group, humphed. "Whatever it is, can't be good."

All five of them stood side by side, trying to see down the dark corridor outside their cell.

Squinting didn't help as Althea peered into the darkness beyond. She closed her eyes and strained to hear better. There, a shuffling sound somewhere in the distance. Her eyes popped open. Not that there was anything to see.

But a hissing noise followed by metal screeching punctuated a low, steady hum.

The undefinable noise grew.

Althea squashed the surge of hope starting to rise. *Hang on, girl. You aren't saved yet.*

Now the distant ruckus grew louder and was close enough for her to figure it out. It was stomping footsteps mixed with grumbling headed their way. She glanced at the other women. A mixture of hope and fear crossed their dirty faces.

Stretched seconds passed, making the escalating fear around them more palpable.

Son of a bitch. Get here, already!

Those plodding footsteps came close enough for the prisoners to see what made all that ruckus.

It turned out to be a bunch of short, weird-looking aliens. A small group of them stopped in front of the shimmering force field.

Damn, they were the strangest creatures Althea'd ever seen.

Five or four feet tall, standing on two legs, with six arms, and thick, stubby tails like a beaver. Their faces boasted long snouts with four beady black eyes set low in their sockets just above their snouts. Tiny, round ears were perched on top of their oblong, flat heads. Each wore either long or short pants, but kept their stubby little chests bare, displaying the long, coarse hairs covering their bodies, ranging from light gold to dark blue. All of them had an assortment of weapons and at least three sets of handcuffs.

Althea's heart sank. She doubted these guys were there to free them. Great, they were swapping one jailer for another. She'd bet they were going to end up in a place far worse.

And the dorky aliens weren't subtle about getting the neon-red robot out of the way. They shoved the motionless metal woman until she fell flat on her back with a dull thud, her hand still raised. The gibbering short aliens wasted no time grabbing the android under her arms and pulling her out of sight. Once she was gone, one of the aliens aimed a small black box at the force field. It emitted a sizzling whine before the field disintegrated.

Now the creature aimed the box at them. With a snarl lifting his lips, he pushed another button, activating the *nutesh* snare each of them wore around their necks.

Searing agony swamped through Althea. She was barely aware of the others dropping like deadweights to the ground next to her as the damn leather collar embedded with spikes delivered a shocking surge of power.

A distant sound of whoops came from the aliens as they poured into the small room, uncaring of any torment she and her friends suffered.

When the pain stopped, it gave Althea a chance to catch her breath. Though the excruciating torture was gone, her body rippled with lingering trembles. These guys might be short little shits, but they were clever enough to plop a gag over her mouth before her brain unscrambled.

Emitting hoots and whistles, they tied her wrists in front of her before she was yanked to her feet. Those six hands on the aliens came in handy, pushing and shoving her and the others, herding them out of the low-ceilinged cell.

When Toni resisted, one creature pointed his gun at her and shot.

The gag over Althea's mouth muffled her squeal. She almost passed out in relief when she realized the laser shot had blasted a hole in the wall next to Toni, instead of killing her. Freaking hell. Warning received.

She was shoved into moving. Good thing they'd gagged her. Otherwise, her teeth would chatter so hard her jaw would crack. Inhaling deeply through her nose, she swallowed the rising terror.

It's going to be okay, Althea. Hold strong now.
Fall apart later.

* * *

After a couple of steps, Althea and the others were forced to run down the corridor. In between being pushed and shoved, she tried to figure out where the short creeps were taking them. There, at the end of the hallway, was an open elevator. Guess that's where they were headed.

The aliens didn't stop, just pushed the women into the cab, smushing them together.

When the upward ride stopped, the doors opened. They weren't in the subbasement anymore, but in a wide room like the lobby of a luxury hotel.

No time to gawk.

Their captors squealed and hissed, shoving and pushing to keep the prisoners running, aiming for the obvious exit at the other end.

It was hard to tell what the room normally looked like, because utter chaos reigned.

Althea had a fleeting impression it used to be a sterile, open reception chamber.

The walls were round and pasty, chalky white that matched the hard concrete-looking floor.

Different aliens ran around, tearing the place apart or fighting.

Littered around were other unmoving neon-colored androids, like the one in the basement.

All were stuck in mid-pose that reminded her of mannequins in an old shopping mall.

And they weren't the only robots stuck. A variety of mechanical droids were lying on the floor. None looked like they had power. Whatever security they provided was long inactivated.

The air was thick with a potent mix of death, excrement, and a strong ammonia odor. Screams filled the room as writhing, organic aliens littered the ground in a macabre dance.

A few unknown creatures dared to challenge their captors, who responded by shooting indiscriminately without hesitation. The victims' bodies disintegrated on impact. No warning, no mercy. Just swift annihilation.

Althea couldn't believe these little shits were so tough. It didn't take long for her and the other women to get hustled out of the building. The tight, two-fisted grip the alien had on her arm was going to leave a bruise. Not that she was stupid enough to struggle and make things worse. Especially since he carried two different rifles in his other set of upper hands.

His lower hands were fisted as he knocked anyone out of his way if they dared get too close.

Once they cleared the building, the bright glare of FiPan's two suns made Althea wince and squint. Her eyes blurred. What she wouldn't give to have a free hand to shade her eyes. As the little asshat pulled her along, she blinked, trying clear her eyesight. She stumbled when a horrible thought popped in her head. Wait, where were her friends? And the rest of the aliens? Instead of being in a group, a single repulsive alien dragged her through a slew of dilapidated buildings on a deserted street.

She'd give anything to dig in her heels and resist, but all it took was her captor showing her the remote to her slave collar in one of his lower hands. Her stomach dropped. With a resigned sigh, she gave in and followed him.

His grip tightened as he dragged her down a grimy alleyway to a small ship.

That couldn't be right. It was a one-seater, like a fighter jet. Where was she supposed to sit?

He led her to the other side of the craft.

Panic set in. The only thing she saw was a small ramp with a coffin-shaped pod sliding down on it.

Before the ramp stopped, the lid lifted until the whole thing became vertical.

"Get's in." The alien gave a guttural demand before shoving her to the pod.

Althea peered into the coffin-shaped cylinder. A wave of nausea made her dizzy. She couldn't imagine being trapped in its narrow confines. Shaking her head, she backed away. "No way, asshole! I'm not getting in there!" Her muffled voice might quiver like a scared little girl's, but she'd be damned if she let that stop her. She balled her hands into tight fists; she'd fight him with everything she had.

The scrawny little runt didn't bother to reply. All he did was press something on the black remote.

The collar around her neck tightened and lifted her off the ground.

"Ack!" she croaked, frantically yanking at the thick leather with ineffective fingers, kicking to get loose. Her jerky movements didn't make a bit of difference.

Smooth as silk, he used the collar to force her inside the unlit cylinder.

Her body was pushed flush against the back. The gag in her mouth dissolved, allowing her to suck in a hard breath through her mouth. She coughed. The air tasted bitterly sharp, loaded with heavy pollutants that made her eyes and nose water.

Alethea scrambled to get out of the pod, but restraints came up and wrapped around her arms, wrists, legs, and ankles. Something cold, wet, and sticky covered the bottom of her feet, creeping its way up her thighs. The sludge slid over her chest and soon reached her neck.

"No!" she screamed as the clear lid lowered. "Sto..." Her last word cut off when the liquid streamed into her mouth. The last thing she heard was the lid closing with a final click. With one last gurgling gasp, she passed out.

* * *

A sudden, biting cold jerked Althea awake from a deep, comfortable sleep. Brain full of mush, it was hard to remember where she was. Then, the memory of being forced into a coffin-like pod rushed through her. With blurry eyes, she shoved at the glass cover above her, desperate to push it open. It dissolved without a sound, and her hands flailed around in thin air.

When she tried to take in a breath, thick slime blocked her lungs. With a heave, she thrust herself over the lip of the cylinder and spewed a thick, clear-orange liquid from her throat and nose. She gasped, scrambling to take in a clean breath. But the viscous liquid lingered and bubbled like acid in her throat. With one last cough, she expelled the remaining blockage onto the floor before sucking in sweet oxygen.

"See-ya!"

The sound of that whiny voice made Althea push a strand of her soggy hair out of her face. She rubbed her eyes in a vain attempt to see better.

"I's tol' ya's I had one!"

Okay, maybe seeing was overrated. Who, or what in the hell, was that? At first, she had a hard time focusing. It wasn't until she wiped the last of the goo out of her burning eyes that they worked. Sort of. She blinked away the last of the fog and spied the creepy little alien with the six arms who put her in the pod in the first place. Who was the freak talking to...?

Her gaze followed the direction he faced and she got the shock of her life. Either she was in some kind of drug-induced hallucination, or she stepped off the reality train and jumped on the choo-choo to Crazyville. In front of the short alien was an honest-to-God anime girl... woman? Come to life. Compete with dusty-pink skin; wide, pink, glowing eyes; flowing fuchsia-and-black hair; all with big boobs stuffed into a Japanese schoolgirl outfit, complete with Mary Jane shoes. Well, that is, if a beautiful anime character had four arms instead of two.

With two of those hands fisted on her trim hips, the other two hands gestured wildly as she spoke. "Covered why girl goo? Drown try to?"

Althea blinked. Huh? What did that bizarre-looking female say?

The little dweeb didn't seem to have the same problem. He spoke in a rush with plenty of finger-pointing from all six hands in unison. First at her and then at the anime woman. "You's-a wanted an Earthing alien, here she is!" He reached over and grabbed Althea by the arm as if to pull her out. "She's-a all's right. Had to keep her under stasis until ready to sell."

"Hey!" Althea yanked her arm out of his hold. At least the orange stuff was good for something. Made her slippery as hell. "Let go, asshole."

"Out's! Let's 'em see ya." The alien pointed to the ground next to the pod hovering above the ground. A stream of the orange goo flicked from his finger and landed between his twitching rounded ears. The line of orange dripped between his beady eyes and rolled down his snout. He used the back of one of his middle hands to wipe it off.

Althea started to crawl out of the now-drained pod, but she noticed she didn't have any clothes on. "Hey!" She squeaked and crossed an arm over her slick breasts. "Why am I naked?"

"Whys yous 'uman's worries 'bout nakked so's much?"

This booming voice couldn't possibly come from the petite anime woman or the short shit next to the pod. Althea swung her head around and gasped. While the alien who took her was shorter than her, this gargantuan male was the complete opposite. The giant reminded her of an old cartoon of Jack and the Beanstalk her grandmother made her watch when she was little.

He had large, bare, flat feet with two split toes that tapered up to trunk-like legs, then a wide set of hips with a bulbous belly. From there, a thin set of shoulders supported his almost nonexistent neck holding a pointed head. His inverted chin drooped with loose skin. His nose was flat over full, rubbery, blush-colored lips that somehow complemented his pale, butter-colored skin. He had one bright-yellow eye with a dark orange, round pupil situated in the middle of his forehead. Saffron goose-down eyelashes framed that eye and matched a single bushy eyebrow.

Holy cow! A real live cyclops.

When she gazed upward, she stifled a giggle. Instead of hair, this guy had a mohawk of lemon-colored feathers sticking straight up in a line down his head like a rooster crown.

"Here's." He flung a loose blanket in her direction.

Althea grabbed it before it flopped over her head. She didn't dare take her eyes off the strange group around her.

"Where am I? Who are you people?" Damn, time to get out of this squishy pod. The remaining orange stuff she sat in was creeping up her fanny and into her exposed lady bits. Wrapping the blanket around her shoulders, she swung her legs over the rim and jumped out. The blanket tried to slide off, but she held it together with a tight fist. Thank God the damn thing reached her knees. No telling how she'd cover up if it was shorter.

"Thanks," she whispered to the giant and cranked her head back to take a good look at him. Shit on a stick. The guy had to be almost eight feet tall.

His one eye blinked as if surprised she talked.

The multi-armed alien fidgeted from one foot to the other. "See's? Nothin' wrong wid her. We's got a deal or what?"

"Arpigig yet not."

Arpigig? Was that the little asshole's name?

The anime girl approached Althea. Her large pearl-pink eyes blazed with white highlights, reflecting some deep emotion hard to figure out.

Was she happy, sad, hungry? Hard to tell with aliens.

"Okay, you is?" Her light, singsong voice was full of concern. She placed a gentle hand from one of her lower limbs on Althea's arm. "Hurt no?"

At least that was easy enough to understand. "Yes, I'm fine." She shivered at the warmth of the woman's hold. It was only then she noticed how cold she was. "Who are you? Why am I here?"

One of the female's hands splayed over her heart. "Hayami I is." She gestured to the gargantuan male behind her. "Flygir mate mine."

Althea's mouth dropped open. This petite little pixie was with that humongous man? That defied physics on a whole other level.

"Dis *puntneji* owes us'es gamblin' monies." Flygir crossed his muscular forearms over his thin chest. "Use's you's paying."

Was he kidding? Intense heat flushed through Althea. She swung around to face Arpigig. "Who the fuck do you think you are? I'm not some toy you can sell off to pay off some damn gambling debt, you jerk." Memories of her duplicitous ex-husband trying to do the same thing flashed through her. She stomped to the alien with a raised fist.

The little dweeb squeaked and backed up, flinging up all six arms over his head and chest as if that would protect him from her fury.

She sneered. She didn't care. He was going down. Yeah, all she needed was just one swift kick right between his stupid stubby legs. That would do the trick. Before she got close enough to make the thought good, four powerful arms held her back.

"No! Let me go!" She tried to pry Hayami's delicate fingers away from her. "I wasn't going to hurt him. Much." Who knew such a tiny little girl was so strong?

"Leave Flygir must Arpigig. Come back never no."

No matter how much Althea struggled, Hayami didn't let go. Hell, the woman wasn't even out of breath.

Flygir picked the little alien up by the scruff of his neck and headed to a wide oval opening Althea hadn't noticed before.

Arpigig squirmed and squealed, trying to pry himself loose from Flygir's firm hold. The giant shook him harder.

"You's lucky Hayami says debt's paid." With a flick of his wrist, he tossed the small creature out. "Leave's an' don' come back. I's won' lis'en to her next time. You's be dead."

It wasn't until the scrawny little alien scrambled away that Hayami released her.

Taking a deep breath, Althea pulled the blanket tight around her and faced her new captors. She drew herself up and thrust her chin out. "Now what?"

Hayami giggled and clapped both sets of hands as she danced from foot to foot. "Pretty new!" she stopped her dance and rushed over to enclose Althea in a tight hug. "Sad more no I."

Althea couldn't make heads or tails of what the woman said, but Hayami's tender expression communicated more than language ever could. For the first time since she'd been snatched from the Exchange, she had a glimmer of hope things might be turning around for her. Heh, maybe the bad luck that plagued her was finally over.

Fingers crossed.

Chapter Two

The desert planetoid Hiigar, just outside the village of Kijiji

Lok stood atop the small dune and surveyed the desolate terrain, his knuckles white from clutching the urn containing his brother's ashes.

It was done. After years of enslavement, the tyrant was gone, vanquished until the only thing left of him was a pile of ashes from last night's funeral pyre. Not a shred of evidence remained of the notorious tyrant who once ruled this corner of the Milky Way. His immense presence that had once been so dangerous and oppressive, was now gone without a trace. All that lingered in his wake were the faint echoes of his terror-filled reign, quickly forgotten and written off as a mere footnote in history.

The wind whispered, cradling the orange-and-gold desert landscape in its wake. A steady breeze nestled through short prickly shrubs as whirling dirt devils attacked the sparse tree line.

On the horizon, the gas giant Omia took up the sky as it danced with the smaller planetoid Gnilia 8SM7, forever caught in its rotation. Low clouds obscured the landscape beneath the dueling planets, giving the illusion rain was coming.

At his back was the blood-orange sun that even in the early morning hours gave off enough heat to make any sensible creature seek shelter.

"Well, Shon." He held the simple metal urn up. The material was so cheap, it didn't cast a reflection. "I hope you finally found the peace you've always looked for."

He closed his eyes. For the first time, he allowed grief to consume him. Taking a shuddering breath, he let the sadness of their wasted lives take over. It hadn't always been that way. When they were young, he and his brother were inseparable. It wasn't until they entered their maturity phase that things took a drastic change. The problem was, Lok always looked like a model Zerin male, while Shon didn't. Lok had a thick head of black hair that a pair of scissors wouldn't dare touch. Unshorn, his sensitive tresses grew healthy and robust. His crowning glory were his dual-colored eyes, a deep-jade inner circle with a lighter apple-green outer ring.

While Lok had inherited the proud Zerin traits, his younger brother did not. Over time, it became obvious that Shon would never grow hair, and his single-colored black eyes remained, giving him an alien appearance.

Lok always suspected his family had some hidden extraterrestrial ancestry they were ashamed of.

Because of these differences, the prestigious U'unk family refused to recognize Shon as one of their own. Through his developmental years, their parents kept him in the background, hidden away from the population. When he started going through puberty, their parents erased all records of their "deformed" child and exiled him to a remote galactic labor camp.

Lok never saw him again until that fateful day thirty years later.

By then, Lok had become the golden star of the political scene in the Federation Consortium. After years of struggling, he was about to be appointed as chancellor by the Galactic Senate and Judicial ruling body.

As the most influential government entity in the galaxy, they had ultimate control over every decision made by the member planets.

But on the eve of Lok being granted this enormous victory, Shon showed up.

Lok closed his eyes and relived that fateful day.

He'd entered his private quarters to get ready to meet everyone at the expected victory dinner to announce his win. He'd dismissed his attendants to get a moment of peace and silence before wading through the craziness of the political arena. Standing in front of a full-length mirror, he studied his appearance to give himself a pep talk.

You've got this, he said with narrowed eyes. *You'll finally make them proud.* He grimaced. Why he cared about making his stern, cold, deceased parents proud puzzled him. They'd died of an incurable disease years prior, making Lok give his word he'd become chancellor after they passed. He thanked the fates they had died together. Living with one parent without the other was impossible to imagine. The hard expectations they'd heaped on him would've turned his life into something unbearable.

Something behind him in the reflection caught his eye. He straightened. It was *him.* Or rather, it was someone who looked just like him.

Lok whirled around and faced the impossible. "Who... what?" It couldn't be. "Shon?"

"Hello, Lok." The impostor moved close. "Remember me?"

Lok's heart raced as he squinted at the man in front of him. While he and his brother had the same facial structure, no one had ever noticed because of Shon's lack of hair and unusual eyes.

"Miss me?"

The sardonic smirk curling Shon's lips made Lok nervous. The glint in his brother's now dual-colored eyes held a maniacal gleam.

"How..." Lok swallowed hard. "Why do you look just like me?"

Shon held his hands behind him and walked in a slow circle around Lok. "Now how would I be able to take over your life if I didn't look just like you? I may be your identical twin, but we both know there were certain, ah, cosmetic things that had to be changed first." He brushed a hand over the top of his long, silky, black locks. "And getting a wig made from a male who didn't need their hair anymore was easy enough." He gave a nonchalant shrug. "Donning ocular-colored lenses made for me was hardly a challenge."

Lok's face twisted into a scowl. No Zerin male would give away his hair by choice. It'd be like chopping off both hands and giving them to somebody else to use. It was even against the law to donate their hair when they died. That only left one option. Shon must have taken it by force.

His brother stepped closer. "The hard part was finding you alone. I can't believe how you're never alone. You constantly surround yourself with other people who fawn all over you. But you don't have to worry about that anymore." He grabbed Lok around the neck with one meaty hand while plunging a needle on the other side. "That's all going to change for the both of us right now."

Lok's eyes widened. He was instantly paralyzed.

"I thought about killing you. Over and over." Shon's heavy breath bathed Lok's face in a rancid odor. "But I guess I'll just have to be satisfied with killing our wonderful parents." His phony sigh never reached the glassy look in his eyes. "My only regret is I didn't make them suffer more."

Suffer more? *Fruk*, their parents died a horrible death. Both contracted some kind of virus that shut down their immune systems and hindered the ability for oxygen to be carried to their cells. Their three-day agony was something he'd never wanted to witness again.

"But killing you is too good for what you did to me." His hand squeezed, making it hard for Lok to take in a breath. "No, now you'll be the invisible one." He sneered. "And with you locked away, I'll slip into your place," he whispered into Lok's ear. "Trust me. No one will even realize you're gone."

* * *

A spinning funnel of dirt jerked Lok out of his musings from the past.

In the fifty years that Shon kept him in isolation, one thing became crystal clear. It was Lok's own fault he'd never found out what happened to his brother after their parents had him banished. As close as he and his brother were when they were young, he should've tried to search for him. But he'd been so caught up in pleasing his parents, terrified they'd get rid of him like they did Shon if he didn't do what they demanded. Meekly, he allowed them take over his life. Everything from what he studied to whom he befriended. If memory served him right, they never left him alone. They kept him under their thumb with constant bodyguards, mentors, and teachers. Even the female they slated for him to marry after he'd won the election had been negotiated before they died.

But in all that time, he should've tried to find his brother. If he had, maybe things would've turned out different. For both of them.

Squaring his shoulders and with shaking hands, Lok pried opened the lid to the urn, not looking at the remains within.

"I'm so sorry, brother mine. I'm sure you ended up the way you did because you felt abandoned. You deserved so much more. At the very least, from me." His throat clogged. "I'll never forgive myself for my role in how things turned out between us. Now you'll be free to find the place where you truly belong." In one powerful motion, he flung open the urn and watched the ashes spin into oblivion on a scorching gust of air.

Once the urn was empty, he dropped to his knees and clawed at the dirt with his bare hands. He dug a hole deep enough to swallow the container that once held his brother's ashes. Unwanted tears streamed down his face as he worked, fogging his vision until the ground was a blur of dark brown and gray. Working by feeling alone, he put the empty urn inside the hole and covered it. He wiped the dampness from his face with a dusty sleeve and stood. Determined, he wiped the dirt from his hands, wishing he could brush the past away just as easily. At last, it was over. With one last lingering glance at the unmarked grave, he turned his back and walked away.

Alone now more than ever.

* * *

Lok waited until the sun set before setting out for his destination—the Galaxy's Pub in the small village of Kijiji. Stopping in front of the place, he paused to take in the shimmering lights over the opening that looked like a jewel-encrusted canopy.

Not that the see-through force field into the bar kept anyone from going in or out. The thing's primary function was to keep the desert dust and pesky insects from mingling with the patrons inside. It also didn't drown out the loud laughter and boisterous conversations of the various aliens crammed into the place.

After being isolated for over fifty years, the idea of entering a crowded room made him break out in a sweat.

"Are you coming in, or you just going to stand there and block the door?"

The sound of the rumbling voice made Lok jump. "*Fruk,* Scekkan. Stop doing that." He growled and crossed his arms, tightening his hands into fists to keep from bolting.

The curling lips on the snout of the monstrous Luzusi exposed her fangs. "Well, I ain't got all day. Are you coming in or not?" She stood with her feet apart and her sizable hands on her trim hips.

"Of course I am. I'm here, aren't I?" Lok took a step forward but stopped when Scekkan raised a palm, her prominent black claws gleaming in the reflective force field.

"You know the drill. State your name and purpose."

Lok stifled the urge to push the Luzusi aside. Taking a fortifying breath, he straightened and dropped his arms. "You know damn well who I am. Why do you insist on asking me every time I come over?"

If he didn't know any better, he'd swear the stoic bouncer smiled.

"Because I can."

He'd considered complaining to the owners how the Luzusi treated him differently from any other patron who came into the pub.

But Flygir wouldn't give a shit, and Hayami would only clap her hands and think the whole thing was exciting.

A movement behind the monstrous Scekkan caught his attention. There she was. The only reason he came out of his private dwelling and endured being in public. He'd only recently discovered her name was Althea, and she was a human female from the planet Earth. Tonight, she wore tight leggings under a knee-length sleeveless tunic. She was serving the tavern's patrons, holding up the large tray laden with empty glasses as she darted in and out between customers. Her toned arms held the heavy platter steady as she lofted it high above her head to dodge someone who stumbled in her way.

Watching her rush around the place made his throat dry. What he wouldn't give to have even a brief conversation with her. But the owners never seemed to let her get near him. One of these days, he'd confront them and ask why. But first, he had to get into the building.

Eying the creature in front of him who stood at least a foot shorter, he gave in and played her game. "Fine. I am T'terlok Shon U'unk, formerly of the planet Zerin. May I gain entrance into your less-than-fine establishment and partake of the joys within?" Nobody said he had to be nice about it.

Scekkan graced him with a regal nod. "You forgot to say, 'And I'm the unsung hero that saved the galaxy.' Come on, admit it. It's no secret we're all free since you buried that the evil piece-of-shit chancellor this morning."

Lok's face heated. No one was supposed to know he kept his brother Shon at the small cabin given to him on the outskirts of town. But no surprise everyone knew. "I didn't kill my brother." He gave a brief nod to the pub. "Your boss Hayami has that distinction." He shrugged. "The only thing I did was to keep an eye on him until he died." The vision of scattering Shon's ashes in the dry desert air would haunt him forever.

"Yeah, yeah. And that's why you are an unsung hero." The female stepped aside and waved an inviting hand for him to come in. "Please enter, most illustrious T'terlok Shon U'unk. You are welcome here."

"Just call me Lok." He mumbled the request for the umpteenth time as he entered with his head down. Keeping his eyes focused on his feet, he somehow made his way through the crowd as he headed to the empty seat the owners reserved for him in the back corner. With every step, he inhaled thousands of spicy, alien aromas. The air was thick with the acrid tang of a dozen species all crammed into the small tavern. He plopped onto the hard seat with his back to the wall and sighed, glancing around. Wow, Hayami hadn't skipped over to take his order. Not that he'd deviate from what he wanted to drink. Food was never an option. He wasn't ready to eat in front of others just yet. Sipping the spicy herbal tea here was hard enough.

Before he had a chance to look for the owner, *she* headed his way.

With calm efficiency, she balanced a tray holding a mug filled with the herbal scent of his favorite tea.

Its soothing aroma filled him with the sense of calm he sorely needed.

She placed it in front of him and stepped back with a wide smile. "Can I get you anything else?"

Her husky whisper sent a shiver down his spine.

Such an innocuous question. Can she get him anything else? He inhaled, taking her womanly scent deep inside. In that instant, everything changed. The one thing he never dreamed would happen to him did. He took in another deep breath and basked in the unfamiliar instinct that overwhelmed him. His senses came alive as her normal female scent, laced with a hint of clean floral notes, drove him to possess... to claim that which was his. Here she was, the only one in the universe with the power to melt the cold stone his heart had turned into.

His TrueBond.

Lok wrestled with his fluctuating emotions, trying to resist the urge to act like an ancient barbaric Zerin. One who swooped in and grabbed his fated one to lay claim to physically, sealing their bond without a second thought. Not that he'd do that. No matter how much he wanted to.

After a hard gulp, he dared to glance at her. Watching her exotic, soft, single-colored brown eyes dilate as she sucked in a breath made his dick twitch. With forced casualness, he put a hand on his lap, trying in vain to keep the damn thing from expanding further. Damn, it'd been so long since he responded to any type of sexual stimulus, it was hard to concentrate. He lowered his eyes and gulped through a dry throat. "No, this is fine." He rasped the words. "Thank you."

"Okay."

The hairs on the back of his neck stood on end as her sultry whisper caused a shot of electricity to course through him. He fisted his hands and struggled not to grab her. Vivid images of being alone with her in his desolate cottage flooded his brain. There, in complete privacy, he could indulge in the tantalizing things he longed to do with her. Far away from this place.

"If you want anything, anything at all, please let me know."

Agh. By the Goddess of Life, he'd better not look at her. If he did, he'd take up her innocent question in a way he was sure she didn't mean.

She stood there a heartbeat longer before turning around and sauntering away.

When he was certain enough time had passed, he snuck a glance at her alluring backside. The gentle sway of her hips made his traitorous dick twitch again. Ignoring his body's response, he continued to watch her until the crowd swallowed her up.

With a heavy sigh, he jerked his fingers open and grimaced at the bloodied crescent-shaped imprints his nails had created on his palms. Grabbing the napkin she left, he nonchalantly wiped the blood away, making sure he folded the linen so the stains wouldn't show.

He pulled his glasses out of the breast pocket of his shirt. He doubted he had enough sense to read anything on the tablet he'd brought with him. But at least it'd make him look like he was doing something instead of sitting there like an idiot, staring into space. Too bad he had nothing like his glasses to put over his heart. Maybe then it'd be clear to the traitorous organ that the beautiful human female couldn't possibly be interested in a nobody like him.

TrueBond or not.

* * *

Damn, every alien in Kijiji must be here tonight. Althea had to pay special attention to every step she took as she skirted around the pub, balancing a tray of drinks in one hand while keeping a palm out to avoid colliding with anyone. A part of her was thankful for the previous human employee who taught aliens that tipping was a good thing. It made serving the motley creatures easier. They didn't grumble after they ate, just left some extra credits without complaining.

But tonight, she worried about two things.

First, with Hayami and Flygir at the neighboring city for supplies, the place didn't have its strongest protectors.

The planetoid Hiigar was on the outskirts of the civilized galaxy, full of rebels, gangs, and criminals.

Thank God they left Scekkan behind.

As a Luzusi from Mapra 3S8, she was a mountain of muscles.

From what gossip Althea picked up, Mapra 3S8 was a planet known for their tough, barbaric population.

And Scekkan was no exception. The sight of her was intimidating, despite her female gender. She hovered close to six-and-a-half feet tall, with a slick, shiny, silver-colored exoskeleton that sparkled beneath the bar's soft lighting. Covering her muscular legs were a pair of pitch-black pants, and her black, sleeveless top clung tightly to her body, showing off her toned, alien physique. Her muscular arms appeared to be made of tough, sturdy cords and the long and sharp claws jutting from her fingertips gleamed like blades.

Scekkan rarely cracked a smile.

Althea couldn't tell if the Luzusi even know how to.

Her face remained a stern mask, complete with a rugged jawline tapering to a short snout. Bright-yellow eyes glowed in the low light of the bar, and a spiky, navy-blue Mohawk topped her head.

On her first day there, Althea watched the alien bouncer lift a massive table with one hand as she dispersed a bar fight with the other without breaking a sweat. For fun, without batting an eye, she'd throw anyone out who so much looked at her sideways. Her strength was superhuman, and she had no qualms about using it. She kept order in Galaxy's Pub effortlessly.

Even with Scekkan there, it made Althea nervous that this was the only enforcement in the place. All it would take was one hearty laser blast, and bye-bye, bouncer.

The second thing that made her heart pound and sweat gather on her palms was hoping *he* showed up.

The bewitching alien man had such beauty that one glance made her heart skip a beat, like a preteen with her first crush. After that first sight, he consumed her every thought, his features seared into her memory.

His long, black hair shone like raven's wings and framed his majestic face with liberal strands of gold interwoven into a thick braid that reached his ankles. A straight nose above full, kissable lips gave him a regal air.

It didn't happen often, but whenever he smiled, a hint of his straight, pearly, fanged eyeteeth snuck out.

But it was the dual-colored irises that captivated her.

The inner circle boasted a deep-emerald color with a light apple green around the outer ring.

While the colors were luscious and rich, it was the air of sadness they carried that tugged at Althea's heart.

When he'd first come into the Galaxy Pub, she drilled Hayami and Flygir on who he was.

Flygir's typical answer was, "Don's knows, don's cares."

Damn bulky Orisha was a male of few words.

All Hayami did was squeal and clap her two sets of hands as she jumped up and down, making her pink hair and her ample breasts bounce. "Yes, hero Zerin is. Here glad male is I am." She gushed about him in her singsong voice.

That's all either of them told Althea about him. It took a couple of days before she figured out the guy's name wasn't Zerin. It was the name of his species. Huh, he was one of those aliens who were supposed to take her to the Exchange, the place where she should've found the love of her life. Like that went as planned.

No matter how much she begged and pleaded with Hayami and Flygir, they wouldn't even tell her his name. Fine. She'd find out for herself. Which wasn't as easy as it sounded. Her employers never let her get near the guy. They both ran interference every time she tried to approach the quiet male. Even to take his order.

Once he settled at the small corner table by himself, Hayami would skip over and take his order.

Every time, he asked for the same thing in a low rumbling voice that made Althea shiver, even across the room—a hot, non-alcoholic beverage.

Then, without another word or looking around, he'd put on a pair of reading glasses and study a transparent pad he brought with him. He only spoke in low whispers to Hayami when she brought his steaming beverage or when she asked if he wanted more. As if his words were a rare commodity.

Althea'd covertly watch him whenever she could. He had a habit of lighting up a small pipe until a soothing plume of gray smoke curled in the air as he read. She never once saw him eat anything.

The only thing he did was sit in quiet solitude. From time to time, a brave or drunken wanderer came close and attempted a conversation. If his hard glare didn't scare the alien off, then either Scekkan or one of her patrons would get between them. Which usually did the trick before the alien slunk off. Sometimes with a tail tucked between its legs.

With Hayami and Flygir gone, here was her chance to approach him. That is, if he even came in tonight.

Despite the boisterous laughter and conversations in the pub, the back of her neck tingled. Taking a deep breath, she closed her eyes and turned to the entrance. And... there he was.

He'd dressed in a baggy short-sleeve shirt and pants in a lightweight fabric perfect for the desert atmosphere. Without looking around, he headed for the lone table in the corner the owners left open just for him. With his back to the wall, he sat and pulled out his reading pad. He put on black-rimmed reading glasses, and whatever he read took his full attention.

"Oo-mon!"

It took a minute before Althea heard one bartender calling for her. The damn bug-eyed alien who looked like a pop-eyed fish was flapping his sucker-topped hands, trying to get her attention.

"Geez, Miner-lime. Learn my name, would ya?" If Mnerlime kept bastardizing the word human, she could do the same with his stupid name.

Bubbles popped out of his rubbery mouth before his thin, scaly tongue licked his spittle away. "Take this. Be quick." He held up a heavy tankard with a steaming beverage inside, flapping a finger toward the handsome Zerin.

Oh God. With trembling fingers, she grasped the thick handle of the porcelain mug, put it on her tray, and wound her way through the crowd. *No, don't freak out.* She spoke that litany in her mind over and over. No way was she going to blow this chance. No way. *Get hold of yourself,* she admonished. She glanced around to make sure no one noticed her heart beating so fast it threatened to explode out of her chest any second now. Licking her lips, she focused on him. Everything and everyone else faded into the background. The only thing filling her vision was his strong, square jaw, chiseled chin, regal nose, and full lips. All in stunning, iridescent skin.

As soon as she got close enough, she took in a deep breath to take in his unique scent. One of her hobbies before leaving Earth was blending her own candles. She never lost the habit of trying to identify aromas that made her happy. *Ahh,* he had an underlying flavor of spicy sandalwood, the slightest hint of fresh male musk, with a faint tang of a cinnamon undertone. The unique blend of his remarkable scent was totally new and exciting for her. She swallowed hard and gripped the tankard handle harder. Holy God, no contest. She took in another breath. Damn, she'd found her new favorite.

Squaring her shoulders, she placed the steaming mug in front of him and cleared her throat. "Can I get you anything else?" *Please say yes. Say anything.* She couldn't wait to hear his rumbling voice up close. Even if it was something as simple as a thank you.

When he looked up, she about fainted. Being held in his panties-melting, dual-colored eyes shocked her stupid.

His dark, iridescent pupils expanded, creating a tight ring of emerald and apple green. His lids lowered in a small blink as he took in a deep breath. "No, this is fine. Thank you."

The man's voice had a deep, rich flavor. Totally masculine. Each word a concert in quiet confidence.

He gave a brief nod before glancing down at his drink.

For the first time, she noticed he only had three fingers instead of four, like a typical Zerin. And they were all the same length as he wrapped them around the steaming mug.

"Okay." Her voice came out in a raspy whisper. Damn, her throat was parched. "If you want anything, anything at all, just let me know." Wow, it didn't take much for her inner slut to come out, now did it?

Not that he seemed to care. He gave another nod and swiped something on his tablet, giving it his full attention.

Althea stood there a few moments longer, unsure if she should leave. But then, with a shake of her head, she snapped out of her trance and hurried away. The tingling feeling between her shoulders told her he watched her. Her heart picked up its hard rhythm. Everybody had to hear it, even across the room. No one had ever made her feel so... alive before. His presence had an almost electric charge that drew her in. If she wasn't careful, she'd get lost in it.

Shaking her head to clear away the cobwebs of her wayward daydreams, she lifted her chin and went back to the bar. *Focus, dork. You have work to do.* There were thirsty patrons and tables to be wiped. But later... later tonight, she'd take the stage and sing for him. She had a song ready just for him. Countless hours she'd spent on it, pouring her heart and soul into each and every word. The composition would let him know how he made her feel. Even though they'd never met. She'd only waited for the perfect opportunity to perform it for him.

Until then, every chance she got, she'd sneak a glance at him as much as she could get away with before anyone noticed.

As Mnerlime made the next round of drinks, she pondered what had happened between them. Usually, a guy like him, so cool and detached would intimidate the hell out of her. But was it her imagination, or did his deep dual-colored eyes betray something else? Something hidden? Maybe... admiration? Or, dare she hope, personal interest in her? She wasn't sure, but when he leaned close, he didn't seem as indifferent as he appeared. The sincerity in his eyes betrayed a kind and sensitive soul.

Althea frowned. *Well, dammit.* She forgot to ask his name.

* * *

You're so pathetic. Lok chastised himself. *What are you going to do, eh genius? Run off with Althea before you even introduce yourself to her?* He savored the foreign-sounding name Hayami had gleefully told him the last time he was here. *So stop being a* fruking *coward. Act like a grown man. Find your balls and talk to her when she comes back.*

Trying to be as nonchalant as possible, he glanced around the room until he caught sight of her unusual curly hair as it bounced with each step she took between the tables and chairs, serving her customers. When she turned to talk to a Veslu—a small alien that resembled an invertebrate with six-winged arms and legs and a short tail—he watched how she interacted with the creature. Even though he was too far away to hear what they talked about, her expression and actions said it all.

She gave the three-foot patron a wide, warm smile and nodded before scratching it between its antennae.

The Veslu vibrated in pleasure after she walked away.

An uncharacteristic anger rose inside him. Damn. He swallowed the rage. What in hell was that? His face burned. During all the years he suffered at the hands of his narcissistic brother, he never understood the emotion of envy. Until now. Watching Althea interact with another male, even if the creature wasn't any kind of competition, made him clench his hands to stop from jumping up and pulling his TrueBond away.

From everyone.

Wait, just wait. Soon she'd come back to his table. Then he could act like a grown male instead of an untried youth. Sucking in a growl, he focused on the tablet. At first, the words swam, but he soon became absorbed in the scientific theory of black wormholes used for interstellar travel. Maybe even between galaxies and dimensions. No one had proven it yet, but the underlying general mathematics didn't rule it out. By itself, a black hole was simply a singularity with an infinite density. However, if two connecting ones were found—a black hole and its mirrored twin, also known as a white hole—they might create an interdimensional portal.

The implications were astounding. If they could travel to other dimensions quicker than traveling across their own galaxy, think of the trade opportunities! Good thing his opportunistic brother wasn't around to exploit this. He shuddered, imagining what Shon would've done with this information. Even though it was a wild assumption, Lok knew as chancellor, his brother would have put countless lives in jeopardy just to test the theory. And, as far as he could tell, no one ever solved the fundamental problem of a wormhole's unstable nature...

A loud crash jerked him out of his musing. A group of humanoid males were fighting amongst themselves, pushing, and shoving one another. At least he thought they were males. Hard to tell with the transparent thick shell covering their bodies instead of clothes. Their two eyes covered the sides of their faces and were multi-faceted like an insect, with small holes where their mouths or nose should be. It didn't appear as if they were hurting each another, just smacking each other with their bulky, sausage-like digits, and waving them about as if there weren't any bones to hold them in place.

Scekkan tromped in-between them as they squealed like small children. Without a word, she smacked their heads together and carried their unconscious bodies to the front entrance, throwing them outside.

She pressed a button on her throat and spoke in a low growl for someone to "come and pick the trash up."

It was easy enough to hear what she said since silence rang in the smoky, dim atmosphere of the pub. All eyes were on the bouncer.

"What?" Scekkan barked. "Anyone else want to test me today?"

Boisterous conversations resumed as if nothing had happened.

Lok automatically searched for Althea. There she was, heading to the stage carrying an exotic wooden... thing. What was she doing?

As she passed through the crowd, they became quiet again until she sat on a backless stool on the bare platform. She swung up the hollowed wooden device to rest on her lap.

It had six strings strung across it down a thin neck. In the center was a single, circular hole probably used to amplify sound.

She strummed the strings.

They thrummed with a pleasant, metallic ring.

Ah, it was a musical instrument. He sat back to enjoy the mellow melody until she opened her mouth and sang.

Pure joy tumbled from her.

He got so lost in watching her sing, it took a while before the lilting lyrics penetrated his foggy mind.

All too long I've waited
Waited for you to come into my life
The stars and moon rise and set
Each second a lifetime without you
The galaxies are too small without you
The twinkling stars cannot compare to you
The universe is empty without you
I yearn to touch you, to be embraced only by you
How long will you make me wait?
How long before you hear my call?
How many countless hours do I have to die a little inside without you?

All too long I've waited
Waited for you to come into my life
The stars and moon rise and set
Each second a lifetime without you
Come to me...

With each syllable, she looked him straight in the eye.

He had to resist looking behind him to see if she sang for someone else. No, she wasn't singing to anyone but him. The warmth in her eyes stole his breath away. His treacherous heart shuddered before thrumming with a rush so hard it made his eyes water.

What a stupid reaction for a male to have. Being a recluse for so long made it hard for him to control his emotions around others. But he refused to give in to the urge to be a coward and look away with his head ducked. He had nothing to be ashamed of. And he refused to make this exquisite female think any less of him if acted like that.

So, he met her stare head-on. Pouring all the longing and desire she brought out in him for her to see.

Her voice never faltered, but her single-colored brown eyes widened as a rosy flush coated her rounded cheekbones. She licked her lips and repeated the last stanza with a rolling thrum on the strings that spoke of an unfaltering passion aimed at him.

When her last silvery word faded, the silence in the pub was deafening. As one, the group jumped out of their chairs as a unified cheer erupted. The place was filled with claps, whistles, and hoots of admiration.

With fierce intent, Lok held Althea's stare, his body rigid and throbbing with tension. He slowly rose and bowed, keeping his arms locked against his chest, not allowing the electricity between them to break. He stayed motionless, sending a powerful proclamation of unwavering commitment to his TrueBond.

Chapter Three

J oy sang through Althea. The handsome Zerin not only saw her, but that welcoming look in his eyes gave her the courage to step off the stage and head straight for him. She carefully put her guitar on the stool, never taking her eyes off him.

Looked like the gamble she took to sing that song in public paid off. The countless hours she spent on it was totally worth it. With each lyric, she'd prayed he'd recognize every word was for him. The second their eyes met, everything fell into place.

He was the reason she left Earth. Justification settled within her at all the pain and terror she'd endured up to this moment. One glance into his two-toned eyes made the universe align. For once.

Only a few inches away now...

Her hand just about touched his when a piercing light and sound burst into the room. Ducking, she put her arm up to shield her eyes as screams echoed from the patrons running and scrambling around in panic. When normal light in the room returned, Althea put her hand down and straightened, facing the front entrance.

The shimmering force field was gone, and in its place was a group of the ugly-as-shit aliens who kidnapped her. Hayami had told her their species were called Ozevroc, and their reputation in the galaxy were ones of scavengers who'd sell their own litter for profit.

As if to prove that point, all of them aimed some type of barrel weapon held in their middle hands at everyone in the room.

"Those disgusting *puntnejis* have Bloodspillers." The Zerin's deep baritone rumbled low behind her.

She glanced back. *He* was there. Close enough for his warmth to ease the shivers rolling down her spine.

He put a comforting hand on her shoulder and pulled her close.

Leaning into him was as natural as breathing. "What's a Bloodspiller?" she asked softly.

"A very nasty, illegal weapon," he replied, in an equally quiet tone. "Those weapons have multiple destructive modes that fire armor-piercing projectiles and explosives that are coded to be activated only by the owner. It'll self-destruct if anybody else tries to use it."

The middle Ozevroc put his Bloodspiller on his hip with the barrel facing the roof. In his snout was a long cylinder that looked like it was wrapped with green leaves, with red smoke twirling around the glowing tip.

Flashbacks fluttered by of old movies she watched as a small child with her dad. He'd been obsessed with movies that came out in the thirties and forties, especially the black-and-white gangster films. This guy smoked his stogie like one of those old-school actors from back then.

The alien plucked the smoldering cigar out of his mouth and addressed the room, twirling its smoldering tip around to make a point. "Yeah-a, let's not waste time. Where's Hayami?"

Scekkan didn't hesitate. She stomped through the crowd to face the alien, claws out. Before she got close enough to do or say anything, the Ozevroc next to the leader shot her. Scekkan disintegrated in a puff of ash.

Althea jumped at the sound, her ears ringing from the blaring shot. "Oh, shit." Tears blurred her eyes as she cursed under her breath.

"Yeah-a. You's waz-nt Hayami. I ask's again. Where's Hayami?" The creature stuck the smelly cigar-thing into the side of his snout. He adjusted the crotch of his snug muddy-colored pants with one of his lower hands.

When no one said a word, he took the cigar out and flicked its long tube of white ash on the floor.

"Lis'en peoples, so you knowin' who's who. Le's ge' down to bidness." He turned to his murderous companion on his right. "Citpigig, line 'em up!"

"Yeess, Zurpigig, boss sir." The smaller Ozevroc pointed his Bloodspiller at the crowd as his three other companions followed suit. "Line's up at the bar wid yur limbs in the air." He shoved a couple of the aliens in front of him and waved his gun to the front of the bar. "Nows, you worf-less piece of burnt brains. I not say again!"

As one, everyone in the room held their free appendages in the air and shuffled to the front of the bar.

"Stay close to me." The tall Zerin whispered in her ear. "I'll protect you."

Awe, that was so sweet. Unrealistic, but sweet. Althea wasn't sure how he could protect her with these heavily armed gangsters unless he had some kind of hidden weapon on him.

"It's all right." She took in a deep breath. "I've been through something like this before." She hated admitting that to him, but when her husband of twenty years left her destitute because of an outrageous gambling debt with some unsavory characters, she had no choice but to take employment where she could. And the only place that gave a second look at her empty resume was a convenience store in a bad section of town where robberies were a part of life.

"Doesn't matter." He walked behind her as if to protect her from a gun's blast on her back. "Stay right by me."

Oh, lordy. He was her knight in shining armor. Now all she had to do was live through this shitstorm so they had a chance to know one another. At the very least, she'd like to find out his name before they died. She hummed as she watched the scared patrons line up with no one fighting back. Maybe his name was something regal... like Talon or ooh, Mikhail from one of her favorite paranormal romance series.

Althea's musings were cut short when one of the uglies herded her and the Zerin to the end of the line by waving his weapon at them. That they ended up as far away from the entrance as possible had to be done on purpose. She gave the Zerin next to her a quick glance. His calm demeanor didn't fool her one bit.

He'd somehow maneuvered them to end up where they did.

With a quick peek down the line of terrified customers, she swore she'd never seen such a bizarre sight in her life. What a wild set of sentient beings they were. All of them, in different sizes and shapes, standing there not uttering a sound. Over the last couple of weeks, she'd gotten used to most of them. Even considered some as almost friends. Too bad none of them struck her as the "warrior" type. Nary a solider or law-enforcement sort among them.

With a side look, she considered the tall Zerin beside her again. While his firm and mouthwatering body had a healthy set of manly muscles, she doubted he got them by doing heavy physical training. He struck her as more the studious type. He probably kept himself in fine shape by doing some kind of strenuous yoga rather than chasing bad guys.

She stared at Zurpigig.

He'd stopped in front of the patrons, with one of his bushy eyebrows raised, and gave his first victim a once-over. The red smoldering smoke from his stogie wrapped around his snout as he chomped it between his sharp teeth.

Althea clenched her jaw and bit the tip of her tongue to stop a moan from escaping. Great. Now came the fun part. The assholes would demand something with an impossible time frame. And if they didn't get it fast enough, everyone in the room was as good as dead.

"Yeah-a." Zurpigig towered over one of the small regular patrons at the other end of the line, a Kecil by the name of Olqoid.

The poor thing always reminded her of a platypus. That is, if a platypus was the size of a Shetland pony.

"Lissen up, you's parasitic peasant." Zurpigig grabbed the fluffy fur surrounding Olqoid's neck that had the thickness of a lion's mane. He shook the creature.

The Kecil squealed, and his head wobbled back and forth. His front legs pinwheeled as the Ozevroc held him up.

Which surprised the hell out of Althea, since the aggressor was a tad bit smaller than the alien he held aloft.

"Dis you's know where Hayami is? No's? Oo-tay. Den you's tell me where that assmonkey Arpigig is. He's diss'peared with valuable cargo. You's seen 'em?"

The poor Kecil pissed his pants before his four eyes rolled up. He passed out.

With a puff of disgust, Zurpigig tossed the Kecil's limp form at the hard wall holding up the bar.

After a resounding crack when Olqoid's head hit, he dropped to the floor and didn't move.

Althea made a move to see if he was okay, but the powerful grip from the Zerin kept her in place. She shot a glance in his direction.

He gave a single nod at the lump on the floor.

Moving closer, she saw its chest rise and fall. She whooshed out a deep sigh of relief.

"Yeah-a. L'ess try this again, people. Since Hayami ain't here, I needs to find the criminal Arpigig who's ship is not far from here." He swung the Bloodspiller to the next recipient in line. "But he's no's where in sight. Does you know where 'es gone?" He put the barrel of the gun under the chin of a water-green Uthatochloris.

This alien was a water-based humanoid by the name of Eykirris who was every bad girl's wet dream of a merman on two legs.

Althea once asked him why he was on a desert planet.

He'd given her a winsome smile and answered, "Why not"?

"I know not what you speak of." Eykirris responded in a calm, cool tone. He pushed a lock of his seaweed-green hair out of his brilliant-yellow eyes. "If you would describe this fellow along with the cargo you seek, I'm sure we can come to an understanding."

Zurpigig pulled the destructive weapon away and pointed the barrel up. "Yeah-a." With a smirk curling his snout, he backed up with one of his six hands planted on his narrow hip.

The aroma of the stogie hanging out of his mouth drifted to Althea. She sneezed as the pungent aroma burned her nose.

"Arpigig stole a slave that's mine!" One of Zurpigig's hands waved erratically in the air. He shot a blast from his Bloodspiller, making everyone flinch.

It put a sizable hole in the ceiling through the apartment above.

The hot, dusty, desert air filled the room.

"If that bastard think's 'es gonna sell wha's mine, I'll gut 'im alive. And I's know Hayami and her idiot mate knows every-ting that go's on here. I demand to speak to them right the *fruk* now!"

Oh, hell. Was he talking about her? Althea pressed her lips together. She never knew what happened to the Ozevroc after Flygir threw him out. Hayami and Flygir told her not to worry about him, they'd taken care of the slaver. Especially after she agreed to work for them. She'd planned on staying here for at least a year before deciding what to do with the rest of her life. It was the least she could do to repay their kindness. Not that she had anything else to do. Earth held nothing for her, and it didn't seem like she'd find love at the Exchange like the Zerins promised. She might as well stay here as anywhere else.

Althea took a tentative step forward. Maybe if she offered to contact the owners, they'd spare anyone else getting hurt. Heh, maybe then the jerks would go away.

"I'm sorry, but Hayami and Flygir are off-planet, getting supplies." She'd be damned if she told them anything more concrete. "And they didn't plan on being back for several days."

Zurpigig's bulbous head swung in her direction. "Yeah-a. What's we got here?" His snout curled the closer he got.

"Tha's something ugly." The companion behind him shook his smaller body like a wet dog, his six arms flapping around as if boneless.

Althea bit her bottom lip to keep from spouting something snarky in return. Freaking creature wouldn't win any beauty contests in the American south where she was from, that was for sure.

"That's a oo-mon!" The bartender, Mnerlime, shouted from his hiding place behind the bar.

Well, wasn't he just a fount of helpfulness?

The gangster tilted his head. "Never heard of a oo-mon before's." He nodded and looked her over. "What planet you's come from?"

"She's with me." The handsome Zerin stepped next to her, wrapping an arm around her shoulders.

"Yeah-a. Lookie 'ere. A Zerin." A weird gurgling sound came out of Zurpigig's throat.

It took a minute for Althea to realize he was laughing.

"T-ain't that nice?" His companions chuckled along with him.

The evil sound made the hair on the back of her neck rise.

"So, Zerin. Why's you hanging around this place when you's could be back at you's high flootin' perch on your homeworld?" He tilted his head and glared at him through one eye. "Anyone's be missin' ya?"

She tensed and glanced at the male next to her.

His iridescent skin flushed. "I'm less than nobody." He waved a hand around him. "That's why I'm here."

Zurpigig took the stogie out of his mouth and tossed the smoldering butt on the floor. He crushed it under his heel without looking at it. "Yeah-a. I's get that." He swung his attention back to Althea. "So's, you's oo-man, call and get Hayami back here now."

"You do realize the village of Kijiji doesn't have any sort of communication system?" The Zerin shrugged his massive shoulders. "That's part of its charm." He looked around the room. "It's why most of us are here."

"You's betta be wrong about 'dat, Mista 'Less Than Nobody.'"

Althea gasped when he pointed the Bloodspiller at her.

"Less's try dis again. Or's I's promise she's gonna be next."

Chapter Four

Althea jumped when the barrel of the Bloodspiller poked her hard in the middle of her forehead. With an apologetic glance at the Zerin's direction, she took in a deep breath. "Well, what he said is true." She gave the man next to her a brief nod. "But I can send a distress signal to them."

How ironic. Before Hayami left, she insisted on showing how the emergency beacon worked. Althea paid little attention since she never imagined she'd have to use it. After all, they had the large bouncer, Scekkan. But the main reason she didn't want to use it was she was warned by Flygir it might draw unwanted attention to their small planetoid.

Why take the chance the signal would attract a bunch of unsavory characters here at the edge of the galaxy? Especially if the rumors were true, that the underworld leader called Dred Pirate Maynwaring was dead. The mad scramble to take his place had to be getting out of hand by now.

She eyed the gangster in front of her. Case in point. This guy was either the dumbest criminal on this side of the Milky Way, or had some type of weaponry he wasn't showing everyone. While the illegal weapons he and his cohorts carted around were heavy hitters, unless they blew themselves with up the entire village of Kijiji, none of them would survive Flygir's wrath.

She shuddered. Much less the chaotic melee the Merkaba female Hayami would unleash on their asses. Hayami may look like a harmless little pixie that gave any anime character a run for their money, but Althea'd heard rumors about her to the contrary. Apparently, the female was a general in a mercenary group called the AoA, the Alliance of Assassins. Talk about a badass organization. They made the Yakuza on Earth look like a group of children playing in a schoolyard.

The rumors she'd overheard in the pub only reinforced her decision to stay at the Galaxy's Pub, which had to be one of the safest places in the vast universe.

While most of the women on the *StarChance* spaceship heading for the Exchange had studied the general dynamics of the Federation Consortium, Althea delved into the dealings between Earth and all the other planets within the galactic government. For millions of years, they considered Earth a protected habitat, exempt from any interference. But with everything she'd gone through, it was obvious being a native from there didn't seem to matter anymore.

A lot of gossip around the pub centered on the downfall of the previous chancellor, and the void in the underworld he left. It triggered a surge of undesirables' struggles for power that rippled across the Galaxy.

Althea had enough upheaval in her life, thank you very much. Her desire to leave Earth for a better life hadn't changed, even though the promise of finding true love was as elusive as ever. But at least here at this little nothing of a planetoid called Hiigar, she had a chance to live a safe, if uneventful, life. Best of all, the people here offered her better living arrangement than anything she could hope for back home.

And, to be honest, she didn't give a shit the people she lived with now weren't human. She glanced at one of those aliens by her side. Like this tall, hunky freakin' gorgeous Zerin. *Hmm*, maybe she wasn't going to live that boring life after all. He acted like he knew the song she sang was just for him. And that he was the special someone she'd left Earth to find in the first place.

Zurpigig lowered his weapon. "Yeah-a. Do it."

She felt the warmth of the Zerin moving closer as if to protect her. Without taking her eyes off the gangster, she pulled out the necklace she kept nestled between her breasts. It was a small oval contraption with intricate etchings in silver. Pulling the chain out, she pressed the two sides together until it clicked.

"Done," she said in a hoarse whisper.

"Was' done?" The gangster ripped the necklace from her neck. His snout lifted in a snarl. "I don' hear or see none-ting." He grabbed the back of her head and yanked hard. "You betta not be lyin' ta me, *hysta!*"

Between one blink and the next, Althea got shoved from behind so hard that she fell flat on her ass. At the same time the Zerin knocked the Bloodspiller out of the Ozevroc's grip and clasped him in an unbreakable hold around his neck. He held him there with only one elbow around his neck, gripping his wrist in a tight hold with the other.

"Now is that any way to treat a lady?" The Zerin's rumble was loud in the silent room.

Without a word, the other Ozevrocs circled around the Zerin and Zurpigig with their Bloodspillers aimed at the Zerin's head.

"You's better rethink what you's doin', Zerin." Zurpigig licked a black tongue around his snout, leaving a wet trail along his thin lips. "I's hate to see you lose you's head." His claws gripped the Zerin's arm without drawing blood. "Especially since I's could be hit too." His beady eyes narrowed on his henchmen. "Back off, boys. We's good."

The group grumbled, but lowered their weapons and took a uniform step back.

The tension between Althea's shoulders tightened until a loud pop made her jump. She gasped as the Zerin's bright eyes rolled up and his eyes went half-mast.

He flopped hard to the floor.

Suddenly released, Zurpigig stumbled and pressed a hand to his throat.

Without a thought, Althea rushed to the Zerin's side. "Please, oh please." She wasn't sure who she prayed to, but urged the powers that be to spare the brave man. When she put her hands on his wide chest, she breathed in a stuttering breath and glared at the Ozevrocs. She gripped the fallen man's shirt in both fists. "What did you do?"

Zurpigig wiped his snout with the sleeve of his shirt. Nonchalant and as cool as could be, he picked up his weapon and stowed it in a holster across his back. He then pulled another long stogie out of his shirt pocket as he leisurely stuck it in his mouth without lighting it. "Male shouldn' touch me."

Before she jumped to attack the nonchalant asshat, one of his goons held her down with a firm grip on her shoulder. She plopped back on her butt. "What did you do!" she repeated, not caring that her demand was a shout.

"Nothin', little female." He turned and pointed his unlit cigar at his smirking companion, whose lip curled over his snout and exposed his set of fangs. "Chapigig jus' doin' his duty." Zurpigig clamped the end of the stogie in the side of his mouth and strutted to his captive audience against the bar. "Yeah-a. I's coulda kilt that male, but I didn't. I's makin' a point. Ever-body will be jus' fine as long as I gets wha' I wants." He strolled up and down eying the patrons who hadn't moved. "Nows, since no-body here seems to know any-ting useful, we's gonna wait here nice and quiet like until Hayami and Flygir shows up." He pumped his clawed hand up and down in the universal signal for everyone to sit.

Which they did as one.

The ammonia smell of someone relieving themselves made Althea press her lips together. No one here deserved to be treated like this. "Maybe if you let some of them go, it'd go easier for you." She rested on her heels next to the Zerin, keeping her palm splayed across his wide chest to feel his steady heartbeat. He seemed to be all right, just unconscious. But she itched to grab the medical scanner behind the bar to make sure.

"Yeah-a... no." He cocked his head to glare at his audience. "No one's leaves here. I's give Hayami one standard rotation to show up. After that, one 'o you's dies every click until they's do." Zurpigig sat at the nearest table and pulled his weapon out of the holster and rested the handle on his thigh with the barrel pointing up. "Clean this mess up and gets me some-ting to drink." He pointed a clawed finger at a scattered collection of half-full beverages on the tabletop before pointing at Althea.

Glaring at the Ozevroc holding her down, Althea shoved his hand off her shoulder. She gave the Zerin one last lingering look and rubbed her sweaty palms on her pants. She'd rather bash the jerk over the head with one of those heavy mugs than get him something to drink.

Without a word, she jumped up and glared at the gangster, grabbing as many of the glasses and bottles as she could. "You want anything special?" She bit the inside of her lip. Now, what made her ask that? As if she cared what he wanted. She should just give them the cheapest crap they had. Maybe then he'd choke on it and solve all their problems.

"Yeah-a. Me an' the boys want the best! Megesemur Ale all around!"

The whoop of approval from his men was deafening. The drink Zurpigig demanded was one of the rarest in the galaxy. Made from the venom of a death worm of the same name, and only one or two bottles were brewed every year. Apparently, whoever killed one of those creatures for a few drops of their venom ended up dying from the exposure.

She had to wear special gloves if she served it to anyone foolish enough to pay the exorbitant price for one sip.

Freakin' jerk. Maybe if she gave him the rest of the one bottle they had, it'd kill him. One could only hope.

* * *

Althea was beyond exhausted. She finally had enough. She'd spent most of the last few hours rushing back and forth from the bar to the various tables the kidnappers took over. The gangsters kept the terrified patrons lined up in front of the bar.

They were allowed to sit, but couldn't move except to relieve themselves from time to time. Thank God Zurpigig let several of his henchmen help her put the unconscious Zerin in a quiet corner on the floor behind the bar. At least there he wouldn't get trampled by the rowdy Ozevrocs throwing an impromptu party for themselves—at the pub's expense, of course.

Their so-called leader hadn't moved from the table he'd confiscated. Althea did her best to ply him with plenty of booze and food. Maybe that would give him something to do besides think of other demands or go around hurting someone just for fun. Too bad Kijiji didn't have any sort of police force.

With Scekkan gone, the gangsters had free rein to do whatever they wanted to the place. When new customers tried to come in, one of the goons would chase them away.

At least they weren't looking to hold the whole planet hostage.

"Oo-mon!" Zurpigig bellowed in a drunken tone. "Yeah-a! I needs—" *Belch.* "—more's." He wiggled a heavy tumbler he held in one hand while three of his other hands held various finger foods he continued to stuff into his mouth. The Bloodspiller was kept in a tight grip in two of his hands, keeping the weapon in a steady hold across his lap.

Althea eyed the guy. *Argh.* Freakin' alien wasn't getting drunk enough.

Even after sucking down most of the Megesemur Ale, he didn't pass out. His beady little eyes were steady as ever.

It shocked her when he shared a sip of the expensive brew with each of his henchmen. Not that he let anyone touch the bottle housing the dead body of the Megesemur worm inside.

That treasure he kept for himself. It was only recently he'd capped the bottle and switched to a lesser beverage.

Without a word, she brought over two large buckets of domestic beer. The foaming brew sloshed over the sides as she walked, but she didn't let that slow her down. Stopping in front of the gnarly jerk, she thumped the buckets on the floor and ignored the cold liquid splashing over her feet, soaking the cloth material of her shoes.

"Here ya go." She crossed her arms and scowled. "I'm going on break, so if you need anything, you can kiss my ass." With a flip of her curly hair, she turned and flounced away. Insufferable idiot. She'd rather get shot in the back than cater to that moron for one more second. She'd been running around like a crazy person for hours. She was dead tired.

Fuming, she headed to the back of the bar and leaned against the wall, closing her eyes. With a defeated sigh, she thumped her head against the wall. Crossing her arms, she slid down and sat next to the sleeping Zerin. She leaned back and put one leg over the other at the ankles.

Taking a deep breath, she opened her eyes to check on the man. Earlier she'd placed a pillow under his head and used a small blanket from the supplies behind the bar to cover him. Watching his even breaths, she breathed a sigh of relief. He seemed okay.

His eyes twitched back and forth as if in REM sleep.

Althea adjusted the blanket a little higher to cover his shoulders. Just a couple of minutes of rest was all she needed. Closing her eyes, she let sleep take her away.

* * *

Gradually, consciousness returned to Althea. She snuggled into the cozy warmth close to her back, feeling something heavy draped over her midsection, just below her breasts. With a quiet hum of satisfaction, she intertwined her fingers between the strong ones covering her.

"Lovely lady."

The rumbling male voice feathering over her ear made her shiver.

"Are you here in my arms, or are you just a dream?"

A loud crash and a wailing squeal made Althea jerk and her eyes pop open. The smell of alcohol mixed with unwashed bodies made her nose wrinkle. Her side twitched in pain from lying on the hard surface of the floor, and she wrinkled her nose at the stagnant order. Oh, that's right. She fell asleep behind the bar. She sucked in a breath when a charley horse started in her left leg. With a hiss she straightened her legs, and the pending cramp faded away.

The only thing that made her position bearable was the blanket of warmth pressed against her back. Wait, that couldn't be a blanket. Blankets didn't breathe. Or feel so toasty. Or speak in that sexy, inviting tone.

A set of barf-brown webbed feet, complete with round suckers for toes, shuffled back and forth in front of her before lumbering away. Now the only thing in her line of vision were open cabinets filled with empty glasses and mugs waiting to be used.

When the man behind her shifted and pulled her close, she sucked in a breath. Oh God, it was *him*. The Zerin was wide awake and *very* happy to see her. It may have been a long time, but it wasn't hard to recognize what poked her in her lower back. She moaned and resisted the urge to wiggle her butt in invitation.

"I'm afraid this is no dream," she responded in a low voice. "It's more like a nightmare."

His soft chuckle made goosebumps rise at the back of her neck. "As long as I'm with you, a nightmare would never dare show its ugly face."

This guy couldn't be real. No man talked like that. Her heart sank. Her ex-husband used to make fun of her when she'd gush over a romantic scene in a movie. In a condescending tone, he'd tell her if a man talked like that, he probably had a boyfriend somewhere. No straight man would ever speak or act that way.

Grimacing, she squeezed his hand and twisted out of his hold to sit up with her back against the wall. Pushing the heavy curtain of her curly hair away from her eyes, she braced herself to look at him. Oh lord, just her luck. The first time they had a chance to speak together, and she had to look like hell. Her stupid hair had to be tangled and flying everywhere like she stepped off an amusement park roundup ride.

Holding a section of her unruly tresses, she took in her fill of the man lying next to her. Didn't look like the captivating man next to her had the same hair problem. Lying on his side with his head resting on his palm, he was as gorgeous as ever.

His thick black hair was neat and smooth, and his two-toned green eyes sparkled with life as he stared back.

He seemed so powerful, like a mythical deity disguised in mortal clothing. Damn, what she wouldn't give to taste him, to feel his lips upon hers as she caressed his massive chest underneath her fingertips. She'd always wanted to run her hands over a muscular man-chest like his. To keep from acting like an out-of-control dork, she huffed and tightened her grip on her thick hair. No one had the right to look that lip-smacking gorgeous after being unconscious for hours.

Scrambling for something to say instead of staring at him like a brainless twit, she blurted, "What's your name?" Ha! Good one. About time she pulled her head out of her ass to ask him that.

His slow and sensuous smile made her heart flutter. It was the kind of rich grin that turned heads and made women feel special and appreciated. Like they were the only one who mattered.

He sat up and tossed away the long-forgotten blanket to the side. Taking her hand in his, he brought her knuckles up to his lips and pressed a light kiss there. "My name is T'terlok Shon U'unk. But I would ever be so grateful if you—" He turned her hand over and kissed her inner wrist. "—called me Lok."

He kept his eyes on hers, but deep inside she sensed he feared giving her his name. As if she'd recognize it somehow.

Lok. She turned his name over in her mind. Hmm, it wasn't familiar. But it suited him. At least she had a name for the man she spent most of her time fantasizing about since she'd first seen him. Yeah, he definitely brought out her long forgotten giggly early teen-ness. She gave a bitter smile. How depressing a crappy marriage robbed the romantic dreams right out of her.

Reluctantly, she pulled her hand free from his grasp. Her skin tingled where he'd touched her. *Keep it together, keep it together.* She squeezed her fingers, hoping to keep her expression from looking like a brainless floozie panting after a pretty face. Time to keep her wits and at least pretend to be a grown-up.

"I'm Althea MacGregor from Earth." She searched his arresting features and sighed when she didn't see any sign he was in pain. "Are you okay? How do you feel after those assholes knocked you out?"

Lok looked behind her before his focus came back to her. "I'm fine. They only used the stunner setting of the Bloodspiller on me. I've a bit of a headache, nothing serious." He nodded to indicate the rest of the room. "Anything new going on out there?"

Althea pulled her legs together, bending them at the knees, wrapping her arms around them and rested her head there before answering. "It seems pretty quiet right now." She jerked a thumb toward the main room. "Most of them fell asleep, except for their illustrious leader, Zurpigig. That guy is unbelievable. He drinks like a fish, eats like a pig, but is alert as ever. I don't think he's even taken a break to relieve himself. Just sits there and glares at the front door as if Hayami and Flygir will waltz through any second."

Lok frowned. "I'm familiar with their species, but I've never heard they didn't sleep or reacted to alcohol differently than most sentient beings." His dual green eyes dilated. "I wonder if he's taking some kind of narcotic."

Althea tugged on her lower lip with her teeth. "Why are they so eager to get their companion back? He didn't seem like an intelligent fellow to me."

He scooted closer and leaned toward her so that their heads were mere inches apart. "Are you the 'cargo' they're looking for?" His whisper was soft.

She sat straight and searched his face. Did he mean to tell the Ozevrocs? Would he sell her out?

Her thoughts must've been loud and clear on her face because he grasped her and pulled her onto his lap, holding her head between his massive hands. "I would never, ever put you in harm's way. I only ask so that I can protect you better. You can't tell them you're who they're looking for." He gave her face a little shake. "You understand? I know for a fact the Ozevrocs would do anything to rule the underworld in Dred Pirate Maynwaring's place. And finding a rare and unusual beautiful female for the slave market would only help them. We're just lucky that bartender mispronounced the name of your species like he did."

Althea couldn't help it. She chuckled. "Well, Mnerlime is a bit of an ass. But even so, I doubt anybody would describe me as a beautiful female."

Lok leaned back, a puzzled frown creasing his delectable lips. "I don't know what you mean. Why would you say something like that about yourself?"

She snorted. "Look at me! I'm a woman past her prime with a little extra luggage on my ass and hips." She waved a hand up and down her torso before pointing to her face. "Let's not forget the mileage stamped on my face. Every line and wrinkle was hard-earned, let me tell you. So, you see, I'm not the young-and-nubile female most males would want to have sex with. Much less if they had to pay for it."

The handsome Zerin male gripped her arms and pushed her away to look her full in the face. His frown deepened. "It's hard to hear you say that. You are the most alluring, sensuous female I've ever seen. While young women have their own strengths, nothing compares to an intelligent, mature female who knows her own mind."

His seductive eyes searched her face.

"You have an inner beauty that's just as captivating as your physical one. It radiates like a beacon, drawing in any male with your soft, alluring glow. And from the moment I laid my eyes on you, you've held me hostage." He cupped her face between his hands again. "I realize you don't know me very well, but I assure you, I'm going to do my damnedest to protect you from what's going on here. I'll never let them hurt or take you. Understand?"

Althea took in a deep breath, taking comfort in his earnest expression. Coupled with the fact Hayami treated him with unusual deference made her relax. Maybe, for once, she could trust her instincts for the opposite sex. She gave him a tentative smile and nodded. "Yes, okay." She put her hands over his. "I would like to get to know you better." The admission came out in a soft voice.

Again, that sexy smile came out to play. "I can't think of anything I'd like better." He glanced around before leaning back against the wall as he hugged her close. "How about I tell you a bit about myself. Believe me, it won't take long."

She rested her head against his firm pectorals, laying her hand on his shoulder. Her heart soon matched the mesmerizing beat of his.

"As you probably guessed, I come from the planet Zerin..." Lok's soft voice began.

He proceeded to tell her a fantastic tale of his twin brother, the former Chancellor U'unk. For years, the male had plotted to overthrow the democratic Federation Consortium and turn it into a dictatorship ruled by him alone. Recently, though, his evil scheme was exposed, spurring an election of the new chancellor.

Due to his brother's subterfuge and careful manipulation, Lok had been imprisoned for fifty years prior to this event. Far from the eyes of those in power who initially elected him as chancellor.

With downcast eyes, Lok admitted that over the years it humbled him when no one ever noticed he was gone, replaced by someone else. When Shon reverted to his original form years later, it didn't matter that his brother replaced him. Everyone had forgotten all about him by then. It wasn't until U'unk's diabolical scheme was uncovered that the Zerin royals located him again.

His brother's plans were abruptly stopped when he was hit with a Void Bolt he threw at someone else. Embedded in the weapon was a vicious MindWipe, a virus that decimated U'unk's mental faculties and reduced him to a soulless husk.

Lok explained it was his duty to take care of his sibling during his dying days.

"His mind finally shut down last night, and his body soon followed. He took his last breath in the middle of the night."

Lok rubbed a hand up and down her arm. "I scattered his ashes in the desert this morning. Maybe now he'll find the inner peace he'd always searched for."

Spellbound, Althea quivered speechless on his solid lap. Every word he spoke was more heartbreaking than the last. Her eyes flooded with tears. She experienced his pain as if she endured it right along with him. Her head spun as her world shifted, her heart opening like it never had before. The intensity from the man in her arms unsettled her, making her vulnerable. But at the same time, an unfamiliar feeling coursed through her, giving her strength she'd never dreamed possible. Her emotions careened from one extreme to the other and threatened to overwhelm her.

But one thing was for sure. She didn't have enough strength or desire to stop herself from falling in love with the man.

* * *

An ear-splitting clang made the woman in Lok's arms jump. Her delicate body trembled as she grasped his shirt with tight fists.

Boisterous laughter and the sound of someone getting slapped followed.

She moved as if she meant to get up and confront whatever was going on the other side of the bar.

As if he'd let her put herself in danger. "It's okay." He waved a finger to encompass the room. "I don't think they hurt anyone. Listen." He cocked his head as he gazed into her exotic, single-colored brown eyes. A reign of silence continued. He glanced up to make sure no one came back there to join them. He took in a relieved breath when nothing happened.

The only one with them on this side of the bar was the Crinkrid that Althea called Miner-Lime. He lay on the bar top with his head resting over his folded arms. The other two aliens who tended the bar had long since passed out across from them.

"See, it's all quiet. I think everyone is taking some downtime." He chuckled. "I believe you humans call it the calm before the storm."

Althea gave an indelicate humph. "Yay for us." She shifted on his lap.

He schooled his features so she wouldn't notice how much her movement excited him.

"I only hope Hayami and Flygir get here before these cretins kill anyone else. Poor Scekkan." A shimmer of tears gathered in her eyes. "She didn't deserve to die like that. Assholes." Her last word cracked as her light-tan face turned splotchy under the smattering of brown dots across her nose.

If he wasn't mistaken, humans called them freckles. What he wouldn't give to kiss each and every one of them to stop her delicate features from twisting into sorrow. The one thing living in forced isolation taught him was how to recognize what he could control and what he couldn't. Giving her comfort was something he could do.

"Being a Luzusi, Scekkan was proud to die a warrior's death. She was killed defending those she'd sworn to protect." In a bold move, he reached over and brushed some of her shiny, bouncy curls out of her downcast eyes.

She let go of her tight hold on her hair, dropping her hand onto her lap.

He lightly touched her chin and brought her eyes up to meet his. "You wouldn't want to take that away from her, would you?"

The flush on her face deepened. She shook her head. "No, I guess not. But, still."

"If it makes you feel any better, just imagine what will happen when Hayami does come back." He clasped her small hands in his. "Almost makes you feel sorry for the assholes, doesn't it?"

A loud snore echoed in the quiet room on the other side of the bar.

Her lighthearted giggle loosened the tightness in his chest.

"Yeah, I guess so." She turned and looked across their small section at the sleeping bartenders.

Lok took that opportunity to watch her. It was a relief when she didn't recognize his name. There were those in the galaxy who'd like nothing better than to take revenge for Shon's crimes on him. "I know this probably isn't the right time, but I would love to know more about you. All I know is your name. So, who is Althea MacGregor from Earth?"

She shrugged, causing her curly hair to bounce and shine in the low light.

He longed to plunge his hands into the inviting tresses as he kissed her full lips.

"I'm afraid I'm not that interesting. Just a woman who'd reached her forties with nothing to show for it. No family. No career. The only daring thing I've ever done was join the Exchange. I'd hoped to find a new life with a fresh start."

Her self-deprecating chuckle made him frown.

"And look where that got me."

"What is this Exchange? I'm not that familiar with it."

"Really?" She pulled back and gazed at him. "You, being a Zerin, should know all about it."

He rubbed a gentle circle over her back. "Remember, I told you I've been in isolation for the last fifty years. Please indulge me."

"Oh, I'm sorry. I forgot." She settled back and rested her head on his chest.

Her feminine warmth brought an alluring scent that was all woman... all her. Her musky aroma coated his nose, and he itched to explore more. His nostrils flared as he inhaled deeply. The conviction she was his TrueBond settled something deep inside him. He closed his eyes and rested his head against the hard wall and allowed himself to fall into her narrative.

"Well, I can only tell you what they told us on the spaceship, the *StarChance*. Apparently, your people created what they called the Exchange, along with other members of the Federation Consortium, to help those worlds in the galaxy in desperate need of females. It seems like a lot of systems find themselves low on females due to failing genetics, or viruses, or some other reason, making them scarce." She chuckled. "The prince of your people made a deal with someone on Earth to only offer this program to those women who read science-fiction romance on their e-readers. That way, they'd attract open-minded women like me to consider leaving their homeworld to find true love in space."

"Why Earth women?" Lok couldn't remember a time when the galaxy had been short of females. Did that recently happen? He doubted Althea had the answer. Might be a worthwhile research subject to investigate.

When she intertwined her fingers with his, he opened his eyes.

"We were told Earth women are genetically compatible with up to 95% of the humanoid species in the galaxy. And can breed with various species to help them from going extinct."

Her low laugh made his heart tumble.

"What's funny is I recognized most of those species in the Exchange they taught us about. They were all males I'd read about in my favorite science-fiction romances."

Lok frowned. "Last I knew, Earth was a protected habitat that didn't allow anyone near it. Much less be able to monitor anything the population was doing, like what they read. I guess I have a lot of catching up to do." He shifted and snuggled her close. "But tell me about you."

With a long sigh, she continued. "There's not much to say. I met who I thought was the love of my life in high school and married him on graduation day. His family was wealthy, so I never had to work, while he focused on his family business. He was gone often, and I tried to do what I could with a few charities and foundations, but I never did anything serious. For a couple of years, we tried to have children until we discovered he was infertile. We looked into adoption, but he had too many other commitments to put any effort into it. So, that idea died an ugly death."

She sat up and scooted off his lap to sit cross-legged in front of him. She must've felt the need to for the distance to finish her story. "Turns out his being busy had more to do with a deep gambling problem than work. On my fortieth birthday,

I got the shock of my life. Desperate to escape some gangsters he owed a lot of money to, he sold our house and drained our bank accounts. He left me a note saying he paid the dangerous men he owed the money to and that they shouldn't bother me. Then he disappeared, leaving me destitute. Because I didn't have a work history, the only job I could find was in a bad part of town." Her low chuckle was without humor.

She pulled the hair from the side of her face and tucked it behind her exotic round ear.

"The goons he owed the money to weren't happy with what he gave them and turned to harassing me, insisting I had to know where he was. Their threats got so bad, I was afraid they'd end up killing me."

Her delicate shoulders shuddered.

"So, when the opportunity came for me to leave Earth and find true love, I jumped at the chance."

She pushed the sleeves of her shirt above her elbows. "On my way to attend the Exchange, the liaison between the Zerins and the Earth women on the ship took me prisoner and gave me to one of those assholes." She poked a thumb to indicate Zurpigig and his friends on the other side of the bar. "I have no idea how we ended up here. He'd kept me in stasis until he ran up a huge debit with Hayami and Flygir and used me to pay them off." Her luscious lips twisted into a self-deprecating sneer. "Just my luck. Looks like I was destined to end up as payment for someone's gambling habit anyway. Guess I can't complain. I was lucky enough Hayami and Flygir took me in." She gave him a shy smile. "Where I lost my heart to you, T'terlok Shon U'unk."

"Yeah-a!" A loud shout was followed by a bang on the bar top. Zurpigig glared with glee down at them from behind the counter. "Lookie boys, we's got it! Not only do we's got our cargo... we got the infamous Zerin ever'body's lookin for! Yeah-a! Here's our meal ticket to eternity."

Lok leapt forward and threw himself in front of Althea, rage coursing through his veins. *Dammit!* There was no turning back now that the Ozevrocs overheard their conversation. When Zurpigig's snout curled into a lecherous leer, an icy chill ran down his spine. He steeled himself, ready to protect Althea at any cost.

Chapter Five

"Get'em!"

Lok backed up and trapped Althea between him and the wall. Crouching, he was ready to take on the aliens. "Stay back!" He growled. *Fruk!* Good going. He'd been so enamored with Althea he hadn't paid attention to make sure no one overheard them. It was all his fault she'd end up at the mercy of those cutthroat aliens.

The Ozevroc threw his head back and laughed. "Yeah-a! You's no threat, Zerin. Grab 'em both." Zurpigig pounded an open palm on the wooden bar again. "Bring 'em around here." He thumbed behind him to the middle of the room. Two of his cohorts flanked Lok and Althea on one side, while two others followed up on the other. All four pointed their Bloodspiller weapons at them.

Looked like he had two choices. He could attack the four aliens surrounding them and die before he took a single step. Well, that wouldn't help his TrueBond much. Option two, he could gather her under his arm and protect her the best he could as they faced the aliens. No contest. Option two.

"Stay next to me," he whispered, leading her to the middle of the room.

"I'm fine. Don't worry about me." She grabbed his free hand in a tight grip.

He admired the brave front she put on. Here was a woman fearless enough to look danger in the face while looking calm. He hadn't met many who could do that—male or female. Every moment he was with her, his estimation for her rose.

He stopped them in front of Zurpigig.

The other Ozevrocs were right behind with their weapons focused on them.

With a gleeful growl, Zurpigig walked around them, with his lower hands clasped behind his back and the cigar clamped at the side of his mouth. He stopped next to Althea and leaned in.

One of the Ozevrocs behind Lok shoved the barrel of his weapon at the Zerin's lower back.

Lok didn't dare move as the heat from the metal seeped into the fabric of his shirt. It was the only warning he got before Zurpigig backhanded Althea. Instinct had Lok jerking to grab her. He stopped when the alien with the Bloodspiller at his back pushed his weapon deep into Lok's spine.

The smaller alien gripped his arm, his claws stabbing deep enough to draw blood.

Lok sucked in a breath and let his arms drop, standing immobile.

The Ozevroc didn't hit her hard enough to knock her down, just made her head whip around.

Putting a hand on her cheek, she glared at the shorter alien.

Zurpigig pointed his unlit stogie at Althea. "Now's because you weren't honest with us, tings are gonna get a little hard fer the both of ya." He pointed the barrel of his deadly Bloodspiller up and rested the butt of the weapon on his hip.

Lok yanked out of the punishing hold the Ozevroc had on him, ignoring the rip in his shirt and skin to push Althea behind him. He'd not let the *puntneji* near his TrueBond again. He crouched and readied himself to tackle the ass.

"Lok, no..." Althea grabbed his upper arm.

The Ozevroc's chuckle ended abruptly when Lok flashed the fool an evil grin.

The ass might not know it, but he was as good as dead. Even though he'd been in seclusion, Lok kept up with his battle training over the years. Being in isolation hadn't slowed him down.

Lok's gaze stayed locked on the Zurpigig as an oppressive silence settled over the pub. So focused on the creature in front of him, he hadn't noticed the reason the patrons in the room held their breath as they huddled in the corner.

After a few moments it became clear what they were afraid of.

And it wasn't the tension between him and Zurpigig.

Lok straightened and turned around.

In the arched doorway stood an unexpected figure framed by the bright sunshine from outside. The glare made it hard to see any details of the form other than that it was a female.

As his eyes adjusted, it became clear he looked at a Merkaba female—complete with a petite figure boasting a tiny waist and a full breast line, as well as four arms. His eyes widened as he took in the female's figure. At first, he assumed it was Hayami, the pub's owner.

But this woman was far from the innocent-looking, pink, school-girl facade Hayami usually displayed. This one dressed was dressed to fight. In various shades of purple.

A fight he suspected she'd have no trouble winning.

He scanned from the top of her long, lilac colored hair to the last few inches of those thick tresses bathed in a deep pool of magenta that curled past her waist. Wispy bangs crossed the pale-violet skin across her forehead. Covering her generous breasts were twin triangles of barely there blue cloth that tied around her neck and back.

She wore a black animal hide and short, thick jacket with matching fingerless gloves on both sets of her hands. Her black, tight skirt fell just below her rounded bottom, accompanied by black, thigh-high boots with heels so high they'd give any other creature a nosebleed. Poking out from behind her shoulder was the handle of a long katana sword.

Close behind her were two other alien creatures.

One was a Nrgwenya female dressed in a one-piece monokini that barely covered her female assets. She was a Draconian humanoid with yellow-silver feathers over light-colored skin and large-spanned wings on her back. Which were fortunately folded behind her. Clutched in one of her clawed hands was a crystal stave with carved symmetric patterns ending in a curvy twirl at the bottom.

If Lok wasn't mistaken, that staff was an illegal weapon called a Spectral Spire.

Once activated, it disintegrated any organic material it touched.

The other companion was a Sismall male. An annoying creature that resembled a medium-sized rodent with brown tufts of fur on its head between rounded ears. He stood on his hind legs, wearing a one-piece, sleeveless suit with ankle boots. The creature's skinny arms had random brown spots which were also scattered throughout its body and head. True to his species' reputation of being super snipers, this one brought his own deadly weapon—a quadruple laser rifle ironically called a Willbreaker.

Lok had never heard of the three species working together.

The Merkaba female walked confidently into the room and pulled her katana from its holster on her back. Stopping in front of Zurpigig, she pointed the end of her sword at his throat.

Without looking at it, the Ozevroc aimed the Bloodspiller at Lok's chest.

"You." The Merkaba female pointed the sharp blade at Zurpigig's neck.

It scratched a thin line, and a bubble of dark blue blood surfaced.

"I doubt you're the one who sent the distress signal. Now, are you?"

"No, I did." Althea walked around Lok before he had a chance to stop her. "Hayami gave it to me in case of emergencies." She waved at the cowering patrons huddled in the corner, whimpering, and shivering. "And this is an emergency. This guy here—" She pointed to Zurpigig, uncaring he might swing his weapon at her. "—killed Scekkan and kept the rest of us hostages."

"Is that so?" One of the female's thin lilac eyebrows rose as Zurpigig became her sole focus. "Are you that arrogant or that stupid to do something like that in a protected AoA headquarters?" She pushed the sharp tip into his neck until the top embedded an inch into his thick hide. "Don't tell me you didn't see the symbol etched at the top of the front door?"

It wasn't something that anyone could miss before they came in. It was a symbol in old Earth script, with the initials emboldened in black letters against a "blast background" over a sun with a bloody dagger through it, creating a bolt of lightning.

"Everyone who's anyone knows that about the Galaxy's Pub."

A thick line of his navy-colored blood rolled down the blade of the sword before dripping off the side to plop onto the wooden floor.

"So that must mean you're a big fat idiot no one will miss."

"Yeah-a. Le's just take a step back and resolve this like any intelligent creatures, um?" The side of Zurpigig's snout lifted. The unlit stogie fell to the floor. The Bloodspiller he aimed at Lok didn't waver.

Lok had to give the Ozevroc credit.

The male remained cool as could be, even with the promise of death looming close.

"Talk fast." The Merkaba female didn't move a muscle.

"I jus' now found out this here creature is mine!" Zurpigig swung the Bloodspiller from Lok's chest and aimed it at Althea. "One's of my own was suppos' to bring her to us, but he's disappeared. Now's I can't find 'em, so we'll jus' take this here female and be on our way."

The Merkaba threw her head back and laughed. The katana never wavered. "You stupid *rhazin*!" She motioned to the Draconian. "Vovin, show this idiot what we do to his type that kidnaps innocent females, hmm?"

"I'd love to, Shysutá." With an evil grin, the seven foot tall Draconian pulled free an enclosed bag draped over her belt and yanked it open. With a flourish, she dumped the contents onto the floor.

The severed head of an Ozevroc thumped across the floor, gathering momentum, until it crashed to an abrupt halt at Zurpigig's feet. Cold, black eyes stared into space with teeth bared in a final grimace. It rocked momentarily, as if in a final protest against its fate.

Althea gasped. "That's Arpigig, the asshole Aja gave me to."

Zurpigig stepped back, eying the rolling head just as Shysutá leaned forward with a maniacal glint in her eye.

"Did you think you can come into my sister's place and expect to get away with killing people and taking anyone you think is yours?" She leaned in, and a maniacal gleam flashed in her amethyst eyes. "Especially a human she's taken in?" She straightened and *tsked*. "I can't allow such a barbaric practice to happen here, now can I?"

The zing of her katana blade was the only warning before Shysutá lopped Zurpigig's head off.

* * *

Lok had never seen a place empty as quickly as the Galaxy's Pub did. By the time Zurpigig's head flopped to a stop, none of the patrons remained.

Althea let out an astonished gasp and leaped back.

Lok grabbed her and swung her away as the grisly object rolled by her.

"Tukkuttok—" Shysutá eyed the Sismall male and nodded to the bar. "—check on those guys cowering behind there. Get them to clean up this place. I want everything in order within the next hour so we can open back up." She went to a nearby table and grabbed an abandoned rag before shoving the empty containers to the floor. With an elegant plop onto a seat, she used the cloth to clean the navy-blue blood from her sword. Once she seemed satisfied it was as clean as possible, she slid it back into its sheath on her back.

"You got it, boss." The small male strapped his weapon, the Willbreaker, to his hip and scrambled behind the bar.

Shysutá turned to the lithe Draconian female. "Vovin, take the rest of these boys back to their ship." She waved at the small group of Ozevrocs now huddled in the corner abandoned by the bar's patrons.

"Make sure they tell others of their kind that the Galaxy Pub is off-limits. Or we'll make sure it's the last thing they do."

Vovin twittered with a quick nod, smacking her lips. She pointed the crystal Spectral Spier at the group. "Let's go, you *ariuks*. You heard the woman."

The cowering group didn't hesitate. As fast as their short little legs could carry them, they ran out the front door.

"Oh, and Vovin." Shysutá leaned back in the chair and put her feet up on the table. With an elegant flair, she crossed her legs at the ankles. She leaned back and wrapped an arm around the back of the chair next to her. From one of her upper hands, she waved a fingerless gloved finger around her. "After they're gone, take a quick flight round Kijiji and make sure there aren't any others like them hanging around. I'm not in the mood for any more surprises. Done?"

"No worries. I'd love to take care of any kind of surprises like that." The ornery smile twisting Vivin's lips left no doubt she'd enjoy tangling with anybody stupid enough to challenge her. "Just promise me you won't go around killing anybody else. It's my turn, ya know. I haven't had a chance to use my baby for a couple of days now." She patted the stave strapped to her side, with an eager glow in her canary-yellow, single-slitted eyes.

Shysutá smirked. "No promises." Her amethyst eyes turned to look at Lok.

"Humph." Giving Shysutá an indulgent smirk, Vovin sprinted to the front door. Her glorious yellow-and-silver iridescent feathers reflected in the bright desert sun as her wide wingspan unfolded. She was airborne the minute she cleared the doorway.

"So, gorgeous"—Lok became Shysutá's laser focus—"what's your story?" She folded both sets of hands on her lap and leisurely twitched the tips of her toes in a mesmerizing rhythm.

Her nonchalant display didn't fool him for a second.

Lok scoffed. As a leader of the AoA, this female had to know more about him than he did himself. Especially if it involved her sister Hayami, who kept up-to-date with all the gossip within a hundred square miles of the pub. That had to include somebody as infamous as him.

Lok put an arm around Althea's shoulders to bring her close. "Let's not waste time going over what you already know. What's next for us?"

"Okay, if that's how you want to play it." Shysutá wrapped her top set of hands behind her head. "I'm sure you're aware there's an enormous bounty on your head, dead or alive." She shrugged and put one set of her hands on her lap. "Seems like the galaxy wants to see an U'unk's blood spilled. And since they can't do it to that *rhazin* chancellor, they'd settle for you."

"Lok?" Althea whispered. "What does she mean?" She grabbed the side of his shirt and yanked to get his attention. "Why would you have to pay for the sins of your brother?"

Everything around Lok disappeared as he watched her mouth move when she spoke. He wasn't sure what a sin was, but he got the gist of what she asked. "Depending on the crime, in certain Consortium societies, they hold all family members accountable for any individual's actions." He brushed a curl out of her eyes. What he wouldn't give to lean down and taste her. Would her lips be warm and sweet as she yielded to him? He cleared his throat and confessed the hard news. "And I'm afraid Shon's crimes were such that I'm considered liable in several star systems for what he did."

Althea's hold on his shirt tightened. "That's the dumbest thing I've ever heard. That man held you hostage and kept you prisoner for over fifty years. I think you've more than paid the price for being related to that asshole." She stomped a foot. "Damn, I wish I could give your brother a piece of my mind."

No matter how much he tried, Lok couldn't keep from smiling. Althea was obviously naïve about how the galaxy worked. But it would've been something to see her confront his brother. He could see it now.

She'd stand in his personal space and wave an accusing finger under Shon's nose, berating him with moral outrage. Not that it would've done any good. But watching the incredulous look crossing his brother's face would've been well worth it.

He turned his attention to the Merkaba female. "I feel if that's what you intended to do, we wouldn't still be having this conversation, would we?"

Shysutá pulled her feet off the table and stood, slapping the table with a flat palm. "Damn, I knew you weren't just another pretty face, Zerin." She gave a melodramatic sigh, her dark-purple eyes twinkling playfully. "Ah, well... fine. No bounty for us." She chuckled. "Okay, just so you know, when Hayami allowed you to stay here in Kijiji, you came under her protection as well as ours." She clenched her lower hands into fists on her trim hips and paced around him and Althea. Her upper arms crossed over her ample breasts as she tapped her lips with a forefinger. "That's why you're here, isn't it? It's one of the only safe places for you in the galaxy."

Lok gave her a cool look. Damned if he'd say anything to antagonize the mercenary.

"Well, guess I'd better stick around until Hayami and Flygir get back." Shysutá glanced around the now-quiet bar. The only sounds were the bartenders working with the Sismall as they cleaned and swept the floor, straightening the furniture as they made progress. The Merkaba turned her attention back to them. "You both look like shit. Why don't you go somewhere and rest for now? Unless you want to stay and help clean up." She gestured at the empty room.

Lok gazed at Althea's upturned face.

She gave him a slow smile full of promises, not taking her eyes off his. "You are absolutely right"—Althea purred—"we're beyond exhausted." She held out her hand to him. "I have a place upstairs that's perfect for some downtime. Care to join me?"

He wasn't an idiot who had to have his TrueBond ask twice. Closing his hand around hers, he nodded. With a pounding heart, Lok followed her.

Chapter Six

Althea led Lok up the creaking stairs to her little room above the pub. With him so close behind, her stomach twisted in knots. When he laced his fingers with hers, her heart pounded as tingles raced through her that were both exciting and nerve-wracking. To stay calm, she focused on each breath with every step she took. Which didn't help. Especially when he closed the distance between them.

The allure of his natural musk made her lightheaded. Her lips parted, letting his scent seep between her lips. Damn, he made her teeth ache. As his steps came into sync with hers, he brought with him a blanket of warmth she was dying to snuggle into, making it hard to think or do anything else. Trust her to have such a bizarre conflict with herself. Somewhere between anticipation and the hint of losing herself when she was finally with him.

"Lights, dim," she whispered after they crossed the threshold.

The interior's computer obeyed, bathing the small place in a halo of coziness.

She nervously glanced around the sparse place. The only thing her living quarters boasted was a small double bed, a nightstand, and a round chair she dubbed "the yoga ball". The space-age contraption turned into a comfortable recliner once she sat on it. She hadn't bothered to straighten up before she went downstairs to work. Never in her wildest dreams did she imagine she'd be bringing *him* here. Like this. Getting ready to do what she yearned to do for weeks now.

"Althea." Lok's low voice was right behind her. He touched her hair, his fingertips trailing through its length as he turned her around to cup her face in his hands.

His gaze met hers, and the intensity in the dual-green color of his eyes set her ablaze. She melted, her chest rising and falling with each ragged breath.

Eyes hooded, Lok didn't speak another word as he stole a kiss. His warm lips were gentle on hers at first, before becoming more firm, more intense.

Oh, yeah. This was what she wanted, to revel in his taste. Opening her mouth, she took a tentative lick.

He growled and turned the kiss carnal as his masterful tongue danced with hers.

Shots of electricity set every nerve inside her alive.

His large hands moved to her waist and pulled her close enough for her to feel his hardness roll between them. She gasped and squirmed to increase the pleasure his masculinity caused between her thighs. His powerful hands traveled the length of her body, setting her skin on fire wherever he touched, even through the layers of her clothes. When he cupped one of her breasts, his thumb twirled around her painfully erect nipple. Air, she needed air. He pinched the sensitive nub, and she jerked away from the kiss with a cry.

His growl deepened as he peppered soft, gentle caresses with his lips down her neck.

The sound he made reverberated through Althea, all the way to her toes. Soon, she became lost in the overwhelming heat between them. She had no choice but to tilt her head to the side to give him better access, shivering as his talented hands moved lower, tracing circles around her stomach.

His deft fingers burrowed under her waistband and traced the line of her hip. With each feather-light touch, her skin pebbled in his wake. She keened with delight, wiggling her hips. Each swirl of her hips was to guide him to go where she wanted him the most.

With an answering snarl, Lok tugged her close, raising her up until his hardened length pressed against her swollen clit.

The intense pleasure hit her so hard, a hint of fear swamped her. The sensation brought with it old unwanted insecurities. How could someone like her satisfy someone as extraordinary as him? Not only was she way past her prime, but she was a big fat nobody who relied on the benefit of others for her very life. Who was to say he and everyone else wouldn't throw her away like her husband did when her exoticness wore off?

Before she had a chance to let that fear spin out of control, he set her back on her feet, his lips and tongue tracing her ear. In a low tone, he rasped, "I can't believe someone like you is willing to be with someone like me. Tell me, do you want to be with me?"

She shivered. *Oh, God*. What was he? A mind reader? Pushing her fears away, she concentrated on how he made her feel. The sheer conviction of being in the right place at the perfect time took over. The only question was, could she be brave enough to take a chance and grab what he had to offer with both hands? To tell that stupid nagging bitch inside her head to go away? To ignore the idea she didn't deserve a man like him. A sharp twinge of regret tried to latch on, but from deep within, Althea dredged up some latent courage and gave him the only answer she could.

"Yes, oh yes."

His lips curved into a sensuous, knowing smile. "I'm so glad."

That smile held all the promise and longing she'd ever dreamed of from a man. Her knees weakened.

"Then we'll face the journey together."

The heat of passion from his dual-green dilated eyes was the only thing she saw before he covered her lips with his own. His kiss turned licentious when he cupped the globes of her ass and pressed his hardness against her sensitive nub that blossomed from its protective hood. Just one swipe against that sensitive place started an orgasmic spiral. As Lok's kiss deepened, she arched her back and moaned, rocking against him as those talented hands continued to explore her every curve.

Althea's shivers increased. Nothing mattered but the need his touch built, as she anticipated when he'd finally end up deep inside her. She imagined how his powerful strokes would trigger each screaming nerve searching for completion. For once in her life, she experienced an overwhelming craving for a man to ravish her, to make her his own. How tantalizing was it to discover it wasn't an emotion only found in the romance stories she devoured on Earth? With the right man, the erotic sensations inside her roared easily.

His kiss continued while he caressed her buttocks, kneading the flesh with firm strokes.

She moaned, butterflies twisting her stomach and swirling around until her body tensed with anticipation. Desire pulsated hot and wet between her legs. When he pulled away, she blinked, hoping to clear the sensual fog clogging her brain. His triumphant smile made her giddy as he stepped back and separated them. She stumbled as the cool air hit her.

He took her hands in his. "Come with me, TrueBond."

Althea didn't bother asking about the endearment he called her. She was too caught up in his alluring spell.

His gaze never left hers as he led them to the bed. He pushed the jumbled covers back and laid her down, covering her quivering body with his. Pushing her hair away from her face, he gazed into her eyes until her face heated.

She swore the man saw deep into her soul.

The vibrant green in his dual-colored eyes was reduced to a thin emerald ring as his iridescent pupils dilated and burned with want. Never taking his gaze away, he slowly explored her pliant body through her clothes.

With each clever touch, he left a trail of goosebumps in his wake. There was no getting around how much she wanted the man resting so easily on top of her. He brought out things in her she never imagined she had. Violent, sexual emotions that careened out of control, building into a blaze of passion that sizzled down her spine. Through hooded eyes, she watched him with a mixture of awe and anticipation, caught up by the erotic sensations he stirred. As he leaned in, he closed those captivating eyes and kissed her deeply, his lips soft yet demanding. Lost in a fog of need, her eyes closed as well, allowing her to savor each brush of his commanding tongue.

At first, Althea allowed herself to drown in what he did and passively let him lead their passion. Then it dawned on her. She used to let her worm of a husband call all the shots in bed. But with Lok, she wanted something different, a bit of give and take. Wow, if nothing else, that told her how much his touch affected her. She took a deep breath, and his spicy, fresh, male musk almost sidetracked her. *No, snap out of it, you selfish cow. Don't just lie there. Time to be a partner in this dance.* She struggled to get a clear thought as his every caress threatened to blow out her intent to be a willing participant in their spiraling passion.

Concentrating on releasing the hand she'd been clenching at her side, Althea slid her hand down his back and explored to the end of his shirt to burrow her fingers underneath.

As she did, he growled and broke off the kiss. He glanced down at her, and those hot, dilated eyes trapped her as he slipped open the seamless fastenings to her shirt. His strong, masculine fingers pulled the material apart, exposing her quivering breasts. With his lips pursed, her chest became his sole focus.

"Lok." His name came in a hoarse whisper. A command to let him know she didn't want him to stop.

The alien garments Hayami gave her were a blessing since she never needed to wear a bra for support. Which she was thankful now more than ever. His head lowered, strands of his silky hair brushed over her neck below her ear, and his wicked tongue licked while his sharp teeth scraped, sending her nerve endings into shock. Moving lower, he claimed her nipple, drawing it into his mouth and sending a whole new flood of sensations. Her good intentions of becoming dominant flew out the window. The only thing left for Althea to do was grip the firm globes of his ass, pull him in tight, and groan.

Lok echoed the sound as he kissed and licked her skin, his heat surrounding her as he pushed her to the brink of rapture.

She quivered beneath his touch. *God*, she wanted nothing more than to take this to the next level. "Oh, please. Yes... now."

Lok lifted his head. "Kiss me."

Molten lava pooled hard and low. Her inner muscles rippled and heated at the sound of his voice. His tone was implacable. Commanding. She sucked in a ragged breath and pulled his head down to press her mouth against his.

He in turn expertly caressed the swell of her breasts with his skillful fingers, his mouth on hers full of raw sexual hunger.

His hand kneading her breast pulled away, causing cool air to pebble her skin.

Raising up on one arm, he used his other hand to open the seam to her trousers, all the while focusing on her quivering torso.

Under his intense scrutiny, she flushed and squirmed. It was as if she'd waited for this moment her whole life. She wanted him buried deep inside her. Now.

With a possessive male smile, his hand slid between her skin and the material covering her. His expert touch found her waiting center as he slipped between the folds of her channel and laid claim to the bundle of nerves within.

Althea sucked in a hiss as his clever exploration found where she wanted to be touched the most.

As he pulled his hand out, he then stroked and tugged the nubbin, resuming his kiss at the same time.

Which created a tsunami that tightened low inside and threatened to take over. She whimpered and longed for him to kiss another part of her.

In desperate need, Althea slid her hand between them to caress the massive bulge he sported between his firm thighs.

Lok yanked his mouth away and grabbed her hand in a firm grip.

"I—" Her protest ended when he scooted down her body to reach her now-exposed lower torso. She didn't have time to wonder how her clothes disappeared when his mouth brushed over her sensitive skin. Wanting more, she widened her legs to grant him better access. She stroked his hair with her one free hand. When she tugged on the other one, trying to get free, his grip didn't budge.

"No. Mine."

The harsh sound of his voice created a ripple of fire that nearly sent her over the edge.

He lowered his head to feast on the apex between her thighs. His warm breath fanned over her wet, sensitive skin. With an expert move, he dipped two strong fingers inside her slippery entrance, causing her silken sheath to clench hard.

Pleasure crashed over her with every combined stoke, leaving her a quivering mess. Her head rocked back and forth as she writhed in wild abandon. Wave after wave of rapture rose with each lick of his powerful tongue in tune with the stroke of his fingers inside. Her breath quickened and her skin flushed. The sensations became almost too exquisite to bear.

"I've got you, my *allurena*."

Lok licked the outside of her nether lips, and her swollen, sensitive clit throbbed with eager want.

"My everything."

All coherent thought scrambled as his sensual assault never faltered. With each stroke on the nest of sexual nerves within her, Althea arched like a bow and trembled with her eyes squeezed shut. Short little puffs of breath escaped every time his fingers brushed against her quivering skin. It didn't take long for her to snap. She screamed at the sheer force of her release. Her potent orgasm rushed through her, more powerful than she ever imagined it could be.

Lok hummed and moved away.

Through half-lidded eyes, Althea watched him wrench off his clothes. First his shirt, then his pants. Her eyes widened when she beheld his impressive cock. Long, thick, and steady as it jutted out from the nest of black hair at his groin, which didn't look that different from a human penis.

The mushroomed head was slick, as if it created its own lubrication. He gripped the straining shaft and gave it a rolling tug. "Are you ready for me, my TrueBond?"

While his words were said in a steady tone, Althea had no trouble seeing the vulnerability deep within his dual-green eyes. Freed from doubt, she reached for him. "I don't know what a TrueBond is." She kicked off the remnants of her pants bunched around one ankle and yanked off her ripped blouse until she lay before him completely naked. "But I've been waiting for you my entire life." She thrust her chest out, grabbing the sides of her breasts to push them together in invitation. "Please don't make me wait any longer."

The rumbling growl from Lok was answer enough.

His eyes blazed as he released his massive erection and kneeled between her splayed legs. "By the Goddess of All, you're so beautiful. I can't tell you how much I've wanted you. So much so, it pained me."

Tears gathered as Althea believed every word he said. The only way to tell him how she felt was to show him. Opening her arms, she invited him to her.

Time stood still until he finally lowered his welcome weight on her. Wrapping her arms around his broad shoulders, she kissed him. Twining her tongue with his, she swallowed a gasp as his stiff erection unerringly found her entrance, gliding easily inside.

Breaking their kiss, she threw her head back at the sensation of his wide girth entering her slick channel. She gulped for air. Every push of his trim hips stretched her tight flesh in a campaign for her to accept him. She answered by arching into him. That movement created an undeniable tight fire deep inside. The slight sting of his thickness quickly gave way to the lush sensation of the sensual friction she'd searched for. With each steady drive of his velvet-encrusted steel, her feminine need rose higher, searching for that elusive pinnacle. All coherent thought fled as he rode between her thighs.

Althea gasped and writhed beneath him. For one endless moment, she turned incorporeal, lost in a haze of lust and passion as her body tightened around his thick erection. She became undone when each of his powerful thrusts laid a powerful claim on her.

All at once, it hit. Wave after wave of blinding orgasms barreled through her, turning her inside and out in a merciless, endless streak of pleasure so intense, it came with a bite of pain.

One more powerful push of his flexing buttocks brought him balls deep. With a strangled cry, his hardness jerked as jets of hot semen roared through her pulsating body.

Once again, completion blazed through her womb, racing around her stomach and breasts, in a sensation so intense all thoughts fled. The only thing within her power was to let a strangled whine of joy escape her dry lips. Through the fog of her sated mind, she heard his matching harsh groan as his weight blanketed her.

Together, they were perfect.

Lok nuzzled her neck before he rolled them around until they faced each other side by side.

Panting and exhausted, she was cradled in her lover's arms and draped an arm over his waist, tucking her leg between his. Taking a deep breath, she reveled in the underlying musk of a healthy man mixed with the scent of the sexual completion between them. The silence in the room was only broken by her pounding heart. Enfolded in his arms, she was convinced their two souls were one in this moment of perfect harmony.

Gazing at him, Althea became entranced by the depths of Lok's stare. It didn't take much to recognize this was a unique turning point in her life. The long-awaited change she'd been seeking was within her grasp. Eager to savor the emotion, she softly ran her fingers across his high cheekbones, letting her newfound love and appreciation radiate from every touch. The surrounding air pulsed with a raw, electrified energy she'd never experienced before. It was like the two of them were in sync, the connection between them radiating like a heartbeat of its own.

She continued her exploration of his masculine face, her eyes following where she touched. The slight hint of stubble tickled her hand as her fingers feathered down his jawline. His short beard was so soft and dark, like it had been spun from threads of midnight gold.

"I can't believe this is real," Althea murmured, her voice full of awe. "That you're here with me like this."

Lok smiled, his eyes crinkling at the corners. "I'm as real as anyone gets," he said, his voice like a gentle caress. "For once."

Althea frowned and rubbed her hand over the curves of his muscular upper chest. She couldn't imagine being alone for over fifty years. He must've felt invisible for decades. Her frown deepened when something he said came to mind. "Earlier you called me true something or another. What did you mean by that?" she asked softly as she laid her head on his chest and tightened her arms around him.

Lok's shrug made her smile when he rested his chin atop her head.

At first, he didn't say anything.

She closed her eyes to allow the silence to guide him. In the meantime, she'd wallow in the aftermath of their lovemaking, letting him answer when he was ready.

With her head against his powerful chest, she heard his heart pick up a quick rhythm.

"There is a legend among our people about their TrueBond, the only one in the universe that is a perfect match for them. As many legends do, the stories fade in time until most people view them as nothing more than a fairytale." He caressed her arm, rubbing it up and down.

"But I've seen for myself that isn't so. Apparently, our prince, Qayyum E'etu, has found his TrueBond with a human female. As did the new chancellor and a close friend of theirs." He glanced at her with a sardonic smirk. "Until then, I don't think anyone believed it could happen with an alien race like humans." He shrugged. "Guess we were wrong. As far as I know, those women who joined with the royal family were on the *StarChance* with you."

Althea's eyes widened. "Really?" Damn, wouldn't that be amazing? "But what does it mean to be a TrueBond with someone?" It sounded like something she'd read in the paranormal romance novels she devoured on Earth.

Lok sat up. He fluffed a pillow and leaned against it, pulling her with him.

She snuggled into his side with an arm around his naked waist, putting her leg over his.

"Tens of thousands of years ago, our ancestors were a barbaric lot that almost brought our race to extinction with their violent ways. It is said that the All Father was so unhappy with us, he cursed away our ability to create children. Within one generation, our ancestors almost died out. Taking pity on us, the All Mother stepped in and gave us a slim chance to reverse the curse by creating mated pairs called TrueBonds.

When a male and female who are compatible meet, an instantaneous attraction takes over. The urge to be with that person overrides everything else. And once the pair mate, the MalDerVon scroll appears at the same time on each of them at opposite temples. In the middle of that unique tattoo is what we call the heir crystal, which changes color once the female becomes pregnant."

"That doesn't sound too bad. But I don't understand how a TrueBond stopped your people from staying as barbaric as you claim."

Lok chuckled. "That's where the wisdom of the All Mother comes in. She made it so a Zerin male can only mate with a female who shares his scroll to produce children. His ability to have sex with anyone else goes away. Also, when the couple expects their child, if separated, they will experience life-threatening hardships since the male produces natural secretions within his body that carry necessary hormones filled with rich lipids, calcium, and immunological proteins. If he doesn't regularly transfer these to his pregnant mate though touch, it leads to madness and suicidal tendencies for both parties."

Althea swallowed hard. "But what if one of them can't have children? Does that mean that person would never find a TrueBond?" Her age might hinder her from having children. Would he want to be with her if that were the case?

He rubbed the skin at her temple, allowing her curly mass to slip through his fingers.

She about purred with pleasure with each powerful stroke.

"No, it doesn't work that way any longer. Having children is a bonus, but unnecessary. Thousands of couples are together that either don't want children or cannot have them. Finding your TrueBond has nothing to do with procreating." He nuzzled the side of her neck. "It has everything to do with finding the one person in the universe who completes you."

"On Earth we call that our soulmate," she whispered as her eyes filled. "Are you saying I'm your TrueBond?"

He pulled her up to cover him. Gently, he grasped her head between his large hands, and his iridescent pupils expanded. "There's no doubt in my mind you are my TrueBond." He leaned close and covered her lips with his. His kiss was a vow, a promise of his righteous claim.

She gasped as his lips moved against hers, savoring the sensations flooding through her. His words pounded like a drumbeat inside her head, flooding her with emotional power. Deep within, their connection formed as if every syllable he spoke wove an invisible thread of fate between them.

He was now a part of her as he claimed her soul.

She belonged to him as much as he belonged to her.

With a reluctant sigh, she broke off the kiss and rested her head on his firm chest. The thrum of his heartbeat resonated within her. "What do we do now?" She entwined the soft curls on his chest with her fingers.

He kneaded the column at the nape of her neck under her thick hair. "I'd like to say we could go wherever we want, but unfortunately, what Shysutá said about me is true. Until the bounty on my head is gone, I'll have to keep a low profile wherever I am.

"So, if you want to be with me, we should stay here under AoA's protection with Hayami and Flygir. I have a cozy villa on the outskirts of Kijiji that I'd love to share with you." He tensed under her as if he dreaded her answer.

Silly man. Her decision to stay on Hiigar happened long before she met him. Earth had nothing to offer, compared to seeing Lok's face the first thing in the morning or the last thing before falling asleep at night. Spending the rest of her life with him was everything she'd ever dreamed about. And it didn't matter if she got that scroll thingy on her temple or not. She'd risk it all just to be with him for as long as she could.

"That sounds wonderful." She rubbed a finger around his erect nipple. "Are you sure you want to be saddled with a woman way past her prime who doesn't do anything but wait on tables and sing on stage once in a while?"

"I can't think of anything more perfect." He rolled them over, covering her body with his. He nudged her legs apart to nestle within the cradle there. With ease, he slid his strong erection inside.

Althea moaned at the zing of pleasure his fullness created. Joy surged deep inside her as they reunited and became one again. From this moment on, they'd be far more powerful together than either of them ever could be alone.

And this moment was just the beginning.

Epilogue

Outside Galaxy's Pub at dusk, three weeks later

Abalim glanced at his handheld to make sure he was in the right place. Yep, Galaxy's Pub in the village of Kijiji on the planetoid Hiigar. He looked up and down the deserted dusty street, hoping to see someone, anyone, that could verify if this was the right place. He chuckled. Yeah, like anyone on this goddess forsaken planetoid would know where he was supposed to be.

He eyed the disreputable building next to the two-story structures that was as run-down looking as this one. The only encouraging sign was the symbol of "AoA" prominently displayed in red and yellow across the archway.

"JR15, are you sure this is the place someone claimed they saw one of the missing human women?"

He glanced at the small droid resting on his shoulder resembling an Earth spider. This is if the spider had a green and silver metallic body and four legs instead of eight. The little bot quivered as if afraid to voice an opinion.

"JR15?" Abalim gentled his voice as he addressed the fledging robot. He was careful not to startle the little guy since it'd only operated a month ago. "It's okay. Just access the programming your father installed within you before we left."

It amazed him how two other bots created his companion. JR10 and his "mate", JR11, made a small batch of these machines to help him and his brothers as they scoured the galaxy to search for the missing women kidnapped from the spaceship, *StarChance*. JR10 insisted these little bots call him "father" and JR11 called "mother". How strange the universe had gotten when droids wanted to be parents.

Another shocking thing he discovered was that Earth was "recognized" by the Federation Consortium, the ruling body of the galaxy. While the planet was still in a protected status, the government admitted they offered human women in secret to hundreds of species in the galaxy that faced a severe shortage of females. Finding out why women were in such sort of supply was something he wasn't privy to, but then he doubted anyone else had any idea why that happened, either. His sister-in-law, Inanna, the Queen of Akurn, a brilliant geneticist and a biologist in her own right, offered to look into the problem facing so many humanoid species.

She and her consort, his brother Adapa, agreed to become part of the groundbreaking research team with the galactic body, but before they did, they insisted the human woman missing from the Exchange had to be found first. Only then would the Queen put her considerable talents into finding out what caused the dwindling female problem. To help her work on it with a clear conscience, he and his brothers volunteered to search the known galaxy for the missing women.

It's not like he had anything better to do. Having time traveled over seven thousand years left him and his three other brothers at loose ends. Since Akurn and Earth had become allies, the threat of a battle between them and destroying Earth was long gone. Which left he and his siblings with nothing to do. The four of them were new to the modern world, totally useless with the worldwide cleanup efforts after their close brush with an alien invasion. With their newfound freedom, they needed a goal to help focus on who they were deep inside. And the best way to do that was to give them a purpose. Something they'd never experienced before.

Abalim admitted it was strange to have control over his own future. Even so, he was more than happy he and his brothers agreed to split up to look for those missing women. He might love his brothers, but they'd grown up together, never being alone except at night since they were small children. The freedom to choose his next step without having to consult their small group would be liberating. He'd finally discover who he truly was without worrying about being judged and getting teased if anything he did was considered lacking. Not that he didn't retaliate back. Usually when they least expected it.

"Yes, Mister Abalim, sir. The last known whereabouts of the human known as Althea MacGregor was here at the Galaxy's Pub." Abalim tilted his head, straining to hear what the bot said. His tone was so soft. Damn, he wished for the umpteenth time he could psychically read the bot. But JR15 wasn't organic, so he couldn't. Skipping the whole talking process would make working together easier.

Abalim grunted and didn't correct the bot when he called him "mister". No matter how many times he encouraged the robot to call him by his given name, the little guy just shuddered, agreed, and then call him by the title in the next sentence.

"Thank you, JR15. Appreciate it." Abalim put his handheld computer tablet in his jacket pocket. "Why don't you hide before I go in?"

JR15 squeaked and scrambled to his favorite place under Abalim's dreadlocks at the nape of his neck. It was a perfect place for the droid to settle so no one could see him. His pointy little legs were light enough when he moved, it was like a whisper across his skin.

When Abalim passed through the entrance's light force field, he was greeted by a humongous humanoid male with wide flat feet that tapered up to thick thighs. His gaze traveled up the giant's body that thinned at the shoulders and held a head with a triangle shape. A single large yellow eye surrounded by downy feathers for lashes dominated his features. A row of bright canary-yellow feathers in the shape of a mohawk angled down his skull.

"Are you Flygir?" Goddess, he hoped so. Princess Aimee of Zerin was quite insistent he ask this giant for help once he reached Hiigar.

"Who's yous?"

"My name is Abalim. Princess Aimee said you'd be able to help me."

"*Pretty!* Is where my Pretty?"

This high-pitched squeal came from one of the strangest looking females he'd ever seen. At first glance, he'd swear the petite little female was barely out of pubescence. She wore a simple loose black tie and a white blouse tucked haphazardly in a short-pleated skirt. On her feet were small-heeled black shoes with white thigh-high stockings. Her light pink skin matched her neon bright pink and black hair that floated around her as if it had a mind of its own. The sight of her two sets of arms took him aback. But it was her wide-set pink eyes with shimmering highlights in their black pupils that gave him pause.

Since landing on Hiigar, he kept his psychic abilities under a tight leash. But standing in front of these two, he opened his senses a crack to get a feel for who he dealt with. The male was a creature called an Orisha, while the female was a Merkaba. Waves of intelligence and a personality of iron from them both told him all he needed to know. These were the people he was supposed to find.

With a hand over his heart, he gave a slight bow and pretended he didn't know who they were. "I am Abalim from planet Earth here to see Flygir or Hayami. Are they here?"

"Why's yous want's 'em?" The large Orisha male crossed his arms over his thin, wide chest.

"JR15, please come out and display the video for our hosts."

The bot's tiny pointed feet scuttled from behind his head and rested on his shoulder, shivering all the way. Abalim wished he could send the small thing a psychic sense of calm. The only thing to do was encourage the small droid. "It's alright. Go ahead."

"Okay, Mister Abalim sir. If you say so."

The bot folded his legs under him and opened his top eye until it glowed and transmitted a holographic full-length 3-D image of Princess Aimee. If he wasn't mistaken, the female might have once been a human. But looking at her now, you wouldn't know it. From her sleek brown hair with the wide white stripe now tucked into a loose braid behind her, to her tanned skin that had a slight iridescent sheen to it. Like a human, she had single-colored eyes, but instead of one solid color, hers had an unusual combination of vibrant green with hints of golden-brown flecks. Nestled at her left temple was an intricate tattoo with a clear crystal in the middle. And she had four fingers instead of three, which a normal Zerin did.

"Hi Hayami and Flygir! I hope you guys are doing okay. I sure miss you." The image clapped. "Baby Ryox is doing fine and demands to see Auntie Hayami all the time." She clasped her hands together as a serious look came over her face. "Listen, there were more human women kidnapped from the Exchange than we knew. This is Abalim and we've sent him to find one of them, a woman by the name of Althea MacGregor. We'd gotten a thin lead that she ended up at the Galaxy's Pub like I did. Huh, who'd have thunk that'd happened? Anyway, please help him as much as you can so he can find her. Thanks, and let me know when you can visit again. Love you both to the universe and back!" The image of the Princess gave a cheery wave before it dissolved.

"Miss happy is she Pretty!" The girlish Merkaba clasped her upper hands together while her lower ones wrapped around her slim waist.

It took a moment before Abalim realized Hayami had called Princess Aimee *Pretty* instead of using her name.

"All's right. You's can come in." Flygir gestured with his beefy hand for Abalim to enter the smoky pub. "Sit's there." He pointed to a small vacant table by the stage. "Hayami bring's you's somethin' to drink." Flygir's head whipped around when a loud squeal caught his attention. "You's!" He wagged a thick finger at an escalating argument between two small aliens on the other side of the room. He lumbered off in their direction.

"Yes!" Hayami clapped both sets of hands. "There sit you. Bring I drink like humans do." She skipped away, but whirled around and looked at the stage behind him. "Oh! Sweets, here human you see!" She gave a negligent wave to the female on the stage who'd been drumming on a six-stringed musical instrument.

Abalim glanced at the female, who looked like a typical Zerin. Iridescent light skin, a purple tattoo on her left temple with a clear crystal in the middle. Her rich sable brown hair rested over her shoulders in a sleek cascade of curls. He back sat on the comfortable chair and watched the woman put her instrument down. It wasn't until she tucked some hair behind her ear that he realized it didn't swoop up to a point. Nor did she have just three fingers. She had four.

Her sable eyebrows rose. "Oh?" She looked at him. He was so close to the stage it wasn't hard to hear her. "You're here to see me?" She pointed to herself.

Abalim scratched the side of his scruffy jaw. "Well, I'm looking for a human woman by the name of Althea MacGregor. You wouldn't know where she is, do you?"

Her joyful laugh made him smile.

She stood and looked at someone behind him. "This guy is looking for a human woman named Althea." Her mouth lifted into a wide smirk. "Know where she is?" She walked off the stage, holding out her hands.

Abalim watched as a tall Zerin male walked past him and took the woman's hands. His long midnight black hair, pulled into a braid to his ankles, exposed his pointed ears. No question he was a true Zerin. Each hand boasted three fingers of equal length instead of the four humans had.

The male bent and kissed the females knuckles with a low chuckle before turning to face Abalim. "Hello stranger. My name is Lok. May I ask who you are?"

Abalim stood and clasped his hands in front of him. Taking a chance, he opened his psychic senses just enough to get a feel for the couple in front of him. With a small bow of his head, he introduced himself. "I am Abalim from the planet Earth. And this is my AI companion, JR15." He gestured to the bot sitting on his shoulder. "The current Chancellor and Earth's government have asked us to help search for women taken from the Exchange. From what I understand, this illegal trafficking only became known after they removed the old Chancellor from office."

As Abalim spoke, he reached out with his mind and tried to connect with theirs. How interesting. It was harder to do than usual. They both had very distinct personalities, making it hard to get a good read in their minds. But with gentle probing, he uncovered she was the woman he looked for.

And after mentioning the disgraced Chancellor, a mental image flickered in the mind of the Zerin male lighting the burial pyre of the dead leader. *Hmm*, this guy had to be the twin brother of that man. When he reported back to Earth, he'd reassure the new Chancellor the old one was dead and gone.

"I know I don't look like I used to." She looped her arm through the male's. "But I'm Althea MacGregor."

"You are TrueBond's?" That would explain the change in her appearance. "Congratulations."

"Thanks! I couldn't be happier." She hugged her man and gave him a look of unconditional love. Which made the male's stern expression soften when he did the same back to her.

"I take it you don't want to go back to Earth?" He didn't have to be a psychic to know the answer to that, but still, best to ask. He had to take proof back to his brother, so he'd instructed JR15 to record everything that happened the minute he stepped foot into the Galaxy's Pub.

"Oh, hell no!" Althea caressed Lok's jaw, still gazing into his eyes. "I'm right where I'm supposed to be."

Abalim cleared his throat. He hated to break the spell between the couple, but there were other things he had to ask. "You wouldn't happen to know where any of the other women are, would you?"

"Why don't you sit with this male and see if you can help him? It'll give me a chance to get ready for that surprise I promised you." Lok gave Althea a quick kiss. The nervous excitement rolling off him was easy to sense.

She beamed. "You won't be gone long, will you?" She was like a child excited for the Christmas holiday, something a lot of people on Earth celebrated at the end of the year.

"No, my *bateia*, my everlasting love." The male's voice lowered. "I will never be far from your side."

Oh, by the God An. The last thing he need to be a part of was this overt display of new love. It was bad enough he had to endure it whenever he was around his brother Adapa and Queen Inanna. Not to mention how all five of their sons were in the same situation. It was enough to make him want to tear his eyes out.

Abalim was about to close his psychic senses when an unusual probe tried to worm its way into him. He blocked it, but the impression made his skin crawl. He glanced around the room, but couldn't sense where it came from.

"Oh, good. Hayami has brought us some drinks." Althea's voice jerked him out of his concentration. "Sit, and I'll tell you about the women who were in the same slaver cell with me on FiPan."

Abalim barely remembered sitting, much less what the woman said next. She and Hayami gushed about something, but the only thing he focused on was a sudden thin thread of a disturbing malevolence hidden from sight. There, hovering behind Althea. In the dim light, a fractured glow tapered in and out of sight. Like tiny mirrors catching whatever light it could to claim its reality. But it was the blazing intensity of foul purpose coming off it in waves that gave him pause.

Abalim sent a quick glance in JR15's direction to ensure the little bot recorded the dialogue between him and Althea. Satisfied the droid had everything under control, he allowed his primary consciousness to float free, but left a small part of himself behind to answer when necessary. He focused on the obscure shape and cast a psychic web around it.

Show yourself. Abalim demanded. The creature's intelligence was easy to read. No doubt the damn thing heard him.

You are an interesting creature. A definite male voice answered.

Abalim frowned. He got the impression the alien wasn't talking about him. The thing wisped around Althea and ignored everything else. *I wonder if there are more like you. Yes, yes, there must be.*

Get away from her. Abalim made sure he growled the words.

Look how you were once a different species. The strange being continued to ignore Abalim. *And now you've taken on the traits of your mate. Ah, mate. Is that how you turned from one species into another?*

When Abalim felt the alien seeping into Althea's consciousness, he blasted a psychic wave and shoved the creature away.

No! I said stay away from her!

Now he had the asshole's attention. *You dare to interfere with me?* The surprise in the male's voice was easy to hear. *How odd.*

What, you're not smart enough to recognize a threat when it hits you? A wave of blinding, arrogant anger saturated Abalim psychically. The only way to avoid being sucked into a whirling abyss around the creature was to dig deep inside and stop it from affecting him. He struggled to focus and maintain an open line of communication.

If you are, as you say, the mental voice became sharper with each word. *You will tell me where I can get more of these creatures. These... humans.* Abalim sensed when Althea once again became the alien's focus. *Finally, a solution to a problem that has eluded me for far too long.*

Abalim trained his psychic consciousness on a higher plane to confront the disgusting animal. *I won't allow you to get near her or any other human.*

A hard grasp around his physical throat stopped Abalim from advancing toward the threat. He jerked to get away, but couldn't pry the invisible fingers off.

Listen to me, you sanctimonious insect. For I will allow you this one chance to convince me you are the intelligent, sentient "threat" you claim to be.

The entity slammed Abalim back into his physical body, the choke hold released as everyone in the room froze in place. Disoriented, Abalim rubbed his eyes before focusing on the strange creature gliding around Althea. At first, it was hard to understand what he looked at, but soon the alien solidified. The strange being appeared humanoid with two arms and legs, but that's where the similarities with an organic creature ended. This one had a strange amalgamation of crystals, or glass, or mirrors, in various shades of blue. Its surface had smooth flat panels, but also sharp crystal protrusions jutting out from all directions in various lengths.

When the creature stopped where Abalim sat, he became bombarded with images that sped through his mind at a blinding speed. He shut his eyes, putting the heel of his palms over his lids as if it would help control what was happening to him. Just as abruptly as the images came, they stopped. He lowered his hands and blinked his eyes open. The eerie silence in the room was dense. The only sound was his heavy breathing.

He was sure the demonstration lasted only seconds, but the information left behind was clear as hell. This alien came through a black wormhole from a different dimension where he and his kind, called the Krystalii, had eliminated all other sentient life there and built an undefeated empire. Their goal was to spread their kind in every universe to "purify" them. He was here to determine if this galaxy had the necessary materials to transform the planets into the atoms and the molecules needed to start the nucleation process to make more of their kind.

"You may address me as Lord Baelon." The alien moved close. The warmth coming off him took Abalim by surprise.

Abalim clenched his hands to stop from showing any reaction. Internally, he slammed a psychic shield around his mind to keep the damn thing out. He'd do everything in his power to stop the asshole from getting in his mind again.

"Listen to me carefully, you soiled maggot." The nasty sneer on Lord Baelon's face had to match his own. "I am the beginning and the end of all there is. Follow me and I will save you from all you fear." His hypnotizing voice was a mélange of cries from a thousand voices. "I will lead you to a place where death and sorrow can never find you." He leaned in and whispered as if sharing a secret. "If you follow me, I will allow you to live."

Abalim jerked his head away. "Yeah, sure. I've heard that type of bullshit from assholes like you before, you *fruking* bastard."

The alien straightened. The sneer on his thin lips morphed into a cruel, wide smile. Abalim's stomach drop.

"Just as I surmised. No intelligent life here." The crystal creature took a step back. "However, you have shown me a clear path on something I must accomplish first. I will have my people find those human women you're looking for." He glared menacingly at Althea with his icy blue eyes, radiating an aura of wrath. "This one is a lost cause, she has already gone through a transformation. What I need is a fresh supply of human females to bring Krystaii glory to a whole different level. Once I have them, I shall transform this puny dimension into something of beauty and power. This will be the highest fulfillment of my destiny."

Abalim became Lord Baelon's sole focus.

"And I shall relish the pain everyone in this galaxy will endure as I do it."

He vanished. The last word stretched and echoed in his wake.

Everyone in the room moved, like someone clicked the pause button to resume. Abalim searched with his psychic senses to see if anyone else experienced what happened between him and the crystal threat. No, all was calm.

"JR15, were you able to keep recording what happened between me and that alien while everyone else was frozen?" He said in a low voice to the small green and silver droid resting on his shoulder.

"Yes, Mister Abalim sir." The little bot shivered. "I'm afraid I did."

"Oh, look!" Althea's excited voice caught his attention. "Lok's on stage. Oh my God. He's going to sing." Her hands gripped together so hard her knuckles turned white. "You don't have to do this." The last was said in a quivering whisper. It was hard to follow the dynamics as to why the Zerin being on the stage affected her so deeply. Especially after what he just experienced with the looming threat from the Krystalii.

He sent a gentle probe to Althea and discovered the Zerin had been held in captive isolation for over fifty years. For him to be the center of attention was a huge step for him to make. Abalim admired how the determined Zerin confronted his worse fears to show his TrueBond their love was more important than any phobia holding him back.

Perched on the edge of a backless stool, Lok's fingers moved gracefully over the strings of his seven-chord instrument, producing an emotional melody. The bittersweet lyrics floated through the room with an aching, smoky edge. There on the small stage, his heart-rending words filled the air as he sang of forever, longing to be with the one he loved with a fervent passion.

Abalim sat in awe, entranced by the sound of another man pouring his soul out for his woman. The music washed over him like a tempestuous wave, bringing with it an understanding for the first time in his life how true love was a relentless and unstoppable force. One that could never be defeated. It had a solid strength that couldn't be broken, no matter how powerful the enemies' psychic armaments were.

Peaceful determination washed over Abalim. Armed with a new sense of courage and conviction, he knew without a doubt the crystal alien's threats didn't stand a chance. The mind-hold the alien shared fortunately ended up on a two-way street. He discovered the aliens weren't ready to come through the wormhole en masse just yet. They were in the process of sending out scout ships first. Their directive was to search for the missing human women Abalim and his brothers were sent to find.

Lord "Freak-Show" Baelon somehow planned to use human women to propagate their species in a new, time saving way. Which didn't make any sense. How could humans and the crystal alien possibly be genetically compatible? That'd be something he'd have to talk about with his sister-in-law, Queen Inanna, the brilliant scientist.

But the main thing he was sure of they had a small window of opportunity to come up with a way to stop the Krystalii from expanding their access to this dimension with more than just scout ships.

For now, the main thing he had to do was to prevent those assholes from locating those isolated missing women. He had to do everything in his power to keep them from becoming the extensive experiments the Krystalii planned on making them.

Especially before their Krystalii leader discovered a whole planet of them.

"All That I am to You"

All too long I've waited,
For you to come into my life,
To share my hopes and dreams and find a way to get by,
Waited to give all that I am to you,
The thought of being without you,
It's a thought that I fear,
I know that I need you,
Without you, life is gone.
The galaxy is too small without you,
The sky's too big without you,
The stars don't shine as bright without you,
The galaxy doesn't exist without you.
Since I met you, I've been alive,
You brought me back from the abyss,
And showed me how to love,
My days without you I can't bear,
The thought of being without you,
Scares me like no other fear,
I know that I need you,
Without you I can't go on.

The galaxy is too small without you,
The sky's too big without you,
The stars don't shine as bright without you,
The galaxy doesn't exist without you.
I can't imagine my life without your touch,
Without your guidance and love,
Without your laughter, your smiles, and your kiss,
Without you, I'm nothing, just a shadow of who I could be,
You are my light and my hope,
My heart's desire,
Without you I'm lost in space,
The galaxy is dark without you.
Your love is like a sun,
It brightens the darkness of my life,
It shines through all of my days,
And makes everything seem alright,
Without you, my world would be bleak,
My life would be empty and cold,
But with you, I'm alive,
The galaxy doesn't exist without you.
The galaxy is too small without you,
The sky's too big without you,
The stars don't shine as bright without you,
The galaxy doesn't exist without you.
Without you, the galaxy doesn't exist,
Without you, my life is incomplete,
Without you, I can't find my way,
Without you, I'm lost in space,

But with you, I'm alive,
The galaxy doesn't exist without you.

-Lok's Song for Althea

Also by Keri Kruspe

An Alien Exchange
Chloe's Turn
An Alien Exchange Box Set Vol 1-5
Lok's Love

An Alien Exchange Trilogy
An Alien Exchange
D'zia's Dilemma
Ki's Redemption

Ancient Aliens Descendants
Alien Legacy: The Empath
Alien Legacy: The Shapeshifter
Alien Legacy: The Psychic
Alien Legacy: The Vampire
Alien Legacy: The Mage
Qhasheik's Pod (An Alien Legacy Novella)
Claude & Amata (An Alien Legacy Novella)

Watch for more at https://www.kerikruspe.com/.